Oliver blinked, his ey ⟨W9-BZT-630⟩ **quickly to the darkness. A dark, solid mass was heaped on the tile floor. At first, he thought it was a bundle of coats. But it was too solid, and no one was wearing coats in August.**

His heart dropped to his stomach and a chill rushed through his body as he finally recognized what he was seeing.

A body.

Oliver dropped to his knees, his hands shaking as he reached out to touch the person. Were they dead?

Please, no...

Time seemed to slow to a crawl as his hand closed the distance between them. While he moved, he became aware of other details that he hadn't initially noticed.

White shirt.

Black pants.

Blond hair.

No, it can't be.

Like a scene from a nightmare, Oliver placed his hand on the person's shoulder and rolled them onto their back, exposing their face. His heart stuttered in his chest as he learned the answer to the question he hadn't dared to ask.

It was Hilary.

Dear Reader,

I always enjoy the opportunity to write a book set in the Colton family universe, and this one was no exception. Even though I have only one brother, it's fun to imagine what life would be like with eleven siblings, or what it would mean to have a twin. In Oliver's case, he's one of triplet brothers. I have a son, and he keeps me on my toes—I can't imagine having two more of him running around!

As for Hilary, she's felt a special connection to Oliver from the start. And she's been the only one who could make him reconsider his business-focused ways. It was fun to dive into their feelings for one another as they both transitioned from wishing they could be together to actually trying to make it work. No one said love was easy, though, so they face their share of challenges along the way.

I hope you enjoy the latest installment in The Coltons of Colorado series! As always, thanks for reading!

Lara

COLTON'S BABY MOTIVE

Lara Lacombe

HARLEQUIN
ROMANTIC
SUSPENSE

Special thanks and acknowledgment are given to Lara Lacombe for her contribution to The Coltons of Colorado miniseries.

HARLEQUIN®
ROMANTIC SUSPENSE™

Recycling programs for this product may not exist in your area.

ISBN-13: 978-1-335-73802-8

Colton's Baby Motive

For questions and comments about the quality of this book, please contact us at CustomerService@Harlequin.com.

Harlequin Enterprises ULC
22 Adelaide St. West, 41st Floor
Toronto, Ontario M5H 4E3, Canada
www.Harlequin.com

Printed in U.S.A.

Lara Lacombe earned a PhD in microbiology and immunology and worked in several labs across the country before moving into the classroom. Her day job as a college science professor gives her time to pursue her other love—writing fast-paced romantic suspense with smart, nerdy heroines and dangerously attractive heroes. She loves to hear from readers! Find her on the web or contact her at laralacombewriter@gmail.com.

Books by Lara Lacombe

Harlequin Romantic Suspense

The Coltons of Colorado
Colton's Baby Motive

The Coltons of Grave Gulch
Guarding Colton's Child
Proving Colton's Innocence

The Rangers of Big Bend
Ranger's Justice
Ranger's Baby Rescue
The Ranger's Reunion Threat
Ranger's Family in Danger

Doctors in Danger
Her Lieutenant Protector
Dr. Do-or-Die
Enticed by the Operative

Visit the Author Profile page at Harlequin.com for more titles.

This one is for Bekka.

Chapter 1

This was a mistake.

Probably.

Oliver Colton cut the engine of his rental car and stared across the parking lot at Atria, one of the coziest restaurants in his hometown of Blue Larkspur, Colorado. He always stopped by when he was in town, but it wasn't the delicious food or warm atmosphere that kept him coming back. No, his repeat visits over the last two years were due to a certain blonde waitress with blue-green eyes and a ready smile. It was a silly thing for a grown man to admit, but Oliver had a crush on Hilary Weston, and he didn't want to leave tomorrow without seeing her one more time.

He should have gone back to his suite at the Metropolitan Hotel and turned in early. That's what he'd meant to do when he'd said goodbye to his brothers Dom and Ezra. The three of them had spent a couple of hours together at the Corner Pocket, playing pool and teasing each other. And he had already talked to Hilary when he'd stopped in for a quick bite before meeting his brothers. There was no need for him to be here now, especially since he had a six o'clock flight to catch in the morning.

But rather than satisfy his urge to see Hilary, his earlier visit had left him wanting more.

Normally, Oliver just enjoyed flirting with Hilary when he stopped by. And why not? She was pretty, funny and charming. Flirting with Hilary was a nice way to pass the time when he came to visit his family. As a venture capitalist, Oliver was constantly on the go, meeting with people all over the world. Relationships were not something he thought about; short-term flings were all he had the time or energy to focus on.

But being back in Blue Larkspur for his older brother Caleb's wedding had left Oliver feeling... unsettled. He wasn't unhappy—far from it. He loved his life and didn't want to change anything. Still, as he'd watched his eldest brother, Caleb, and his new wife, Nadine, Oliver had felt an uncharacteristic longing. It didn't help that some of his other siblings had recently paired up as well, including his fellow triplets, Dom and Ezra. Ezra had put up a good front at the Corner Pocket, but Oliver could tell his brother was falling for that widow, Theresa. It was only a matter of time before Ezra was as head-over-heels as Dom was with Sami, too. While the three of them maintained a healthy competition with respect to many things, Oliver was happy for Dom and Ezra to take the lead in the romance department.

So why was he parked outside Atria, hoping to catch a glimpse of Hilary through the large front windows?

"I'm just being friendly," he muttered to himself. And yeah, maybe he did feel a little sorry for his single self tonight. Not in a "looking for a relationship" way, but more in a "wanting the company of a beautiful woman tonight" type of feeling. In this kind of mood, he'd rather see Hilary than sit in his hotel suite alone. Tomorrow things would be back to normal—he'd hop on an early flight to Malaysia and dive back into his work, trying to establish an offshore wind farm.

But tonight? He wanted a distraction so he didn't feel quite so alone. The kind his brothers couldn't provide.

Oliver climbed out of the car and walked across the nearly empty parking lot. Blue Larkspur had grown a bit since he was a kid, but there still weren't many people eating out at 9 p.m. on a weeknight.

The hostess smiled as he walked inside. "Back

again?" Her dark gaze ran up and down the length of his body, her eyebrows lifting ever so slightly as her smile took on a knowing slant. It was clear she had gotten the wrong impression, and in another place and time, he might have turned her misunderstanding into an opportunity.

But not now.

Oliver cleared his throat. "Is Hilary still working?"

The hostess's smile froze for a split second as she realized her mistake. An assessing glint entered her eyes as she nodded. "Let me check her section."

The woman made a show of consulting the table map on her podium, then nodded. "Table for one, right this way."

She grabbed a menu and took off at a fast clip. Oliver loped behind her, trying not to look too eager as she led him to a small table by the far wall. The hostess set the leather-bound menu on his table and cleared away the second place setting across from his seat. "I'm sure Hilary will be with you shortly," she said before leaving.

Oliver ran his hands over the tops of his thighs as an older man brought him a glass of ice water. Anticipation bubbled in his stomach and he fought the urge to turn around in the hopes of catching a glimpse of Hilary before she approached his table. No need to look as desperate as he felt.

"Good evening, sir. May I bring you something to drin—" She trailed off, eyes going wide when Oliver looked up. "Well, hello there," she said, a note of pleasure in her voice. Her body relaxed, her whole demeanor changing from formal to friendly in the blink of an eye.

Oliver grinned as he watched her tuck a stray strand of hair behind her ear. It was a little hard to tell in the dim lighting of the restaurant, but he thought he detected a faint blush on her cheeks.

"Hi," he replied, his eyes traveling across her in what he hoped was a subtle once-over. Her starched white button-down shirt, black pants and the black apron she wore tied around her waist weren't designed to show off her body, but he didn't miss the way the fabric strained a little across her breasts. He had no doubt the long black tie that lay over the vertical line of buttons hid a tantalizing peek of the curves beneath her shirt.

If Hilary noticed his attention, she didn't show it. "I didn't think I'd see you again so soon."

"Disappointed?"

She laughed and shook her head. "Hardly." She held his gaze for a few seconds. "Did you have fun with your brothers?"

Oliver felt a small jolt of surprise at the question. He'd mentioned his plans with Dom and Ezra during his earlier visit, but he hadn't expected Hilary to remember what he'd said. Even though it had only been a few hours since they'd talked, she'd probably made polite conversation with dozens of customers since he'd left. The fact that she'd actually listened to him was a boost to his ego.

"Yeah, it was good to hang out with them for a bit," he replied. "Even though Ezra won most of the games."

"I'm not surprised." Hilary's eyes twinkled with suppressed laughter. "There's no way your older brothers were going to let you win."

Oliver gave her a mock glare. "Whose side are you on?"

"So you came back to soothe your wounded pride with some dessert?" Hilary tilted her head to the side. "Things are starting to wind down in the kitchen, but I can get Jeff to whip up a crème brûlée for you."

Oliver leaned back in his chair, considering the offer. "That sounds delicious," he said. "But I have a better idea."

Hilary lifted her memo pad, pen poised to write down his order. "I'm all ears," she said.

"I'll take two," he said. "To go."

"All right," Hilary nodded. "You must be hungry."

"I won't be eating alone."

Hilary's pen paused for a second, her smile faltering at the edges. "I see." Her tone was neutral, but Oliver knew his answer had surprised her, and not in a good way.

"One is for me," he continued. "And the other is for you."

She blinked, clearly caught off guard. "Um, what?"

"Go out with me." He reached out to gently tug on her tie, untucking the pointed end from her apron. A wicked impulse flared to life—it would be so easy to give her tie a harder yank and pull her into his lap, to take their running flirtation to the next level. But no; he didn't want to embarrass her while she was working.

"When?" The way she asked the short question told him she still didn't quite believe he was being serious.

"Tonight. I'm flying out tomorrow, and I'm not sure when I'll be back in town. Don't make me spend my last few hours here with the echoes of Ezra's taunting ringing in my ears." To be fair, Ezra hadn't been obnoxious about his victories, but Hilary didn't need to know that.

"But… I'm working." Hilary gestured weakly at the surrounding tables.

Oliver glanced around the large room, which at this point was mostly empty. "The dinner rush seems to be over," he pointed out quietly. "Can't you sneak out early?"

She bit her bottom lip, obviously considering it. Oliver knew she wasn't trying to be a tease, but he couldn't take his eyes off her mouth. Heat curled low in his belly as he wondered what she would taste like.

Hopefully crème brûlée…

"Come on," he urged, seeing the indecision in her eyes. "What have you got to lose?"

* * *

Hilary Weston stared down at Oliver, warmth suffusing her body as he looked at her with those gorgeous eyes. They were the pale blue of a winter's sky, surrounded by a darker blue rim that drew her in, making it hard for her to think…

"Hilary?"

She shook herself back to the present. Right. Oliver had asked her out on a date. An actual, *real* date.

Anticipation and nerves bubbled in her stomach, like a fizzy drink that had been shaken. She'd known Oliver for a couple of years, if knowing could be defined as an episodic flirtation whenever he was in town. He always made it a point to stop by and say hello, and his attention made her feel special, if only for a few moments. Still, in all that time, he'd never shown any interest in seeing her beyond the restaurant.

Until now.

Hilary opened her mouth to respond, fully intending to decline his invitation. Atria was her family's business, and the other employees wouldn't appreciate seeing the owners' daughter cutting out of work early.

But before she could say no, her hormones hijacked her brain. "Yes."

A slow smile bloomed on his face, dimples appearing in his stubbled cheeks. "Excellent," he said softly. "Should I wait for you here?"

Hilary shook her head. "I'll meet you around the back."

His eyebrows shot up. "You really are going to sneak out. I like it."

Hilary felt her cheeks warm. His approval shouldn't mean anything, but a small part of her was pleased by his response.

"Give me a minute to grab some desserts," she replied. "How does flourless chocolate cake sound?" Crème brûlée was good, but Jeff would have to caramelize the top. And she didn't want to let her brother know what she was doing.

The tip of his tongue darted out to moisten his lips and she felt her knees go weak. "Delicious."

She nodded. "I'll see you in a few minutes."

Hilary forced herself to turn away and head to the kitchen, her thoughts a chaotic swirl. What was she doing? Oliver Colton was way out of her league! He was handsome, charming, funny...and oh yeah, a jet-setting businessman who was rarely in one place for more than a few nights. His invitation was superficially innocent, but she hadn't missed that spark in his eyes. She was a grown-up; she knew how this evening was likely to end. It would be safer for her to back out, to preserve their flirtatious friendship without adding the complications sex was sure to create.

Except...she didn't want to be responsible tonight.

Her family relied on her to help at the restaurant, and while she was happy to do it, the job didn't leave her with a lot of free time. And she had just started taking classes online for her master's degree in international marketing, which would further crimp her already nonexistent social life. This date with Oliver was likely her last chance to let her hair down and do something fun for the foreseeable future. She wasn't going to pass that up.

Hilary pushed into the kitchen, noting the staff was already starting to close down stations and clean up. Jeff wasn't around, which meant he was probably in his little office in the corner, planning menus or ordering supplies. Hopefully she could get out of here without attracting too much notice…

She grabbed a to-go container and headed for the walk-in cooler. At this time of night, any preprepared perishables were inside, ready for the staff to use tomorrow for the employee meal. Jeff always made it a point to cook for everyone before the restaurant opened. Family meals were a nice way of building camaraderie, and Hilary would be the first to admit her brother was an exceptional chef.

The damp cold enveloped her as she stepped inside the small, insulated room. She spied the chocolate cake on a shiny metal shelf but drew up short as something moved at the far end of the room.

Jeff poked his head around a bank of shelves, clipboard in one hand, pen in the other. "Hey," he said, a note of curiosity in his voice. "What are you doing back here?"

"I'm heading out early tonight, and I wanted to grab some cake before I go."

He nodded. "Study fuel?"

"Something like that."

Jeff walked over while she retrieved the cake from the shelf. There were exactly two slices left. She transferred them both to the Styrofoam container, ignoring Jeff's sound of protest.

"Do you have to take both of them?" he asked plaintively. "I was hoping to have one tonight."

"Sorry," Hilary said, feeling a little guilty. "I have a big paper to write, and I need chocolate." She put a little emphasis on the word *need*, and Jeff shook his head.

"Fine," he muttered. "Feed your hormones. I'll just stay here and starve."

Hilary reached up and patted his cheek gently. "You'll be fine," she said cheerfully.

He snorted. "Whatever."

Her mission accomplished, she moved to the door. "I'll see you tomorrow. Get some rest tonight— you look tired." It was true; her brother's normally bright blue eyes seemed dull, and there were lines of strain at the corners of his mouth and across his forehead.

"I'll be fine." He brushed aside her concern and gave her a forced smile. "Good luck with your paper tonight."

A pang of guilt speared Hilary's heart at his encouragement. She never lied to her family. But neither did she want to explain what she really had planned. Tonight she was going to do something just for herself, and she didn't want to share that information with anyone else.

After grabbing her bag and two sets of silverware rolled in napkins, Hilary pushed open the back door of the restaurant and stepped into the night. A mild breeze ruffled the strands of her hair and carried the faint scent of garbage from the dumpster sitting twenty feet away. Not exactly an ideal spot for a romantic rendezvous...

But where was Oliver? She glanced around, searching for him. The entire back side of the restaurant was illuminated by the yellow glow of the security lights mounted on the roof. Aside from a narrow stretch of paved road and the dumpster at the far end of it, she was alone.

Had he changed his mind?

On the heels of that thought came the sound of a car engine, steadily growing louder. Hilary turned to her left in time to see a dark blue two-door pull around the corner and into the alley.

Oliver stopped in front of her and rolled down the tinted window. "Shall we?" he asked with a smile.

Hilary's stomach did a little flip. How did the man manage to make the alley behind the restaurant and a plain rental car look so sexy? It simply wasn't fair.

She opened the passenger door and slid onto the seat, keeping the chocolate cake on her lap. "I'm here," she said. "What'd you have in mind tonight?"

Oliver's large hands settled on the steering wheel

as he started to drive. "You're going to have to wait," he said teasingly. "It's a surprise."

Hilary settled back into the seat as Oliver reversed out of the alley and returned to the parking lot. "Do you do this kind of thing often?"

He glanced at her as he pulled onto the street. "What kind of thing?"

"You know," Hilary said. "Talk waitresses into sneaking away with dessert and meeting you in narrow, smelly alleyways?"

He chuckled, the low rumbling sound making her skin tingle. "You're the first."

Hilary smiled to herself. She was no fool—Oliver Colton had a reputation as a bit of a ladies' man. She was not, in fact, the first woman he'd charmed. But it was nice to be the focus of his attention now.

If only for one night.

She closed her eyes for a moment, feeling a bit like Cinderella on her way to the ball. Tomorrow she'd return to her regular life of work and school.

But as for tonight? She was going to enjoy herself.

Chapter 2

Oliver turned off the engine of his rental car and fixed his gaze on the door of Atria, feeling a profound sense of déjà vu.

Had it really been months since he'd last seen Hilary?

Logically, he understood that it had been ninety or so days since he'd been back in Blue Larkspur. He hadn't spent the time being idle though; the deal in Malaysia was just about closed, and he'd been making all the necessary arrangements so they could start construction on the offshore wind farm as soon as all the i's were dotted and t's crossed. He was proud of this project. It had taken a lot of time and effort to cut through miles of red tape, but the outcome made it all worth it.

There was a price, though. The long hours and late nights meant he didn't have any time or energy for a social life. He hadn't even called Hilary, despite thinking about her every day.

He hadn't meant for things to move so quickly between them. Despite the reputation he knew he had as a ladies' man, he'd only meant to spend a nice evening with her, maybe end things with a kiss or two. And things had started out well enough. After picking her up in the alley, he'd driven to a secluded outlook outside of town. They'd sat on the hood of the car and looked at the stars, talking and laughing as they'd eaten the cake she'd brought for them.

He'd never experienced anything like it.

The women he usually went out with liked to be wined and dined, an experience he generally enjoyed as well. Much of his free time was spent at fundraising galas or charity auctions, events that were always improved by female company. The ladies he brought with him were pleasant and nice enough, but despite what people thought, he didn't jump from bed to bed. Oliver was quite happy to enjoy light conversation and part with a kiss at the door. It was easier to stay focused on work when he held himself back from the trappings of a relationship, so he didn't try to delve beneath the surface with anyone. But things had been different with Hilary. He hadn't felt like he needed to perform for her, to fit her preconceived notion of how a successful venture capitalist acted. With Hilary, he could just be himself, without any artifice.

They'd talked like long-lost friends, sharing childhood memories, comparing favorite movies and music. He'd told her several stories about his big family and growing up as part of a set of triplets, as well as one of twelve Colton children. He'd even opened up a little about his father, talking about how the man's lies had made it difficult for him to trust people now. Hilary had listened without judgment or pity, letting him speak but never prying for details. She'd shared about her brother, Jeff, and growing up as part of the family business. And she'd told him about her own goals, the life and career she wanted to build for herself.

It had been wonderful. And he probably could have dropped her off at her apartment and left it at that.

But then he'd kissed her.

As soon as their lips had touched, Oliver knew he'd made a mistake.

The problem was, he hadn't cared.

Hunger had roared to life inside of him, a banked fire exposed to oxygen after too long. The taste of her had intoxicated him, made his head spin until his entire awareness had narrowed to just her.

Even now, he didn't remember the drive back to his hotel. They must have walked through the lobby and rode the elevator to his suite, though he had no recollection of any of it. He'd been a man possessed, cutting through anything and everything to have Hilary.

She'd been equally affected. Oliver closed his eyes, recalling the feel of her hands on his skin, the desperate way she'd stripped off his clothes, the urgency of her touch as they'd come together to explore each other.

He still remembered her unique flavor. The sweet tang of her skin on his tongue. Her soft moans, the way her breathing hitched when she was on the edge of climax. The feel of her body gripping his, clamping tightly around him as though to keep them joined forever.

Oliver had never experienced anything like it.

Leaving Hilary the next morning had been torture. He'd wanted nothing more than to stay in bed with her all day, to continue exploring the connection he felt with her. To see if the magic of the night before had been a one-time-only fluke, or perhaps the start of something interesting.

But duty had called.

And he always answered.

Now though? Life had slowed down. His project was in a more secure place, one that didn't require so much of his focus. It was time to turn his attention to the personal, to find out if he and Hilary could revive the spark that had flared between them.

He climbed out of the car and started across the parking lot, feeling a spring in his step that had been lacking of late. Oliver loved his job and truly enjoyed acting as a sort of "Green Robin Hood," seeking out renewable energy projects around the world to fund and promote. But as he watched his siblings find love and happiness, he couldn't help but wonder if there was someone out there for him as well. Settling down wasn't something he was particularly interested in at this point in his life, but he had to admit that the idea of a relationship held a certain appeal. His family certainly embraced the idea. Several of his siblings had paired off in recent months, and even his mother seemed to be moving on with the police chief. What would it be like to know someone cared, would be there to share things with? To celebrate his victories, and soothe away his disappointments?

At the hostess station, he made his usual request for Hilary's section. The place was busy tonight— from his vantage point, it looked like all the tables were full. But it only took a few minutes for the hostess to find a small table squeezed against the wall. Oliver followed the young woman through the restaurant, hoping to catch a glimpse of Hilary before she visited his table.

He took his seat and wiped his palms along the tops of his thighs. A nervous energy filled him, making it hard for him to sit still. He'd imagined this moment many times over the last few months; how she would look, what he would say. Would she be upset because he'd had to leave so abruptly after their night together? Would she understand why he hadn't contacted her until now?

Oliver picked up the menu, more to have something to hold and examine than out of any real curiosity about the food. Hilary's voice drifted over from somewhere nearby, and a tingle danced across his skin. This was it. He was finally going to get to see her, to touch her again.

Anticipation built as he stared at the menu with sightless eyes. If he played his cards right, this initial reunion would turn into something more by night's end. Hopefully Hilary would agree to meet him later, and they could spend time alone together, getting reacquainted in more personal ways.

He was so distracted by the thought that he didn't realize she'd arrived at his table until she spoke.

"Good evening. May I bring you something to drink?"

Her voice washed over him, making the fine hairs on the back of his neck lift in awareness. Oliver lowered the menu and looked up, a smile on his lips.

Hilary stared down at him, a look of disbelief on her face.

"Hi," he said, running his gaze over her.

She was still beautiful, but it was clear she had changed. Her normally bright eyes had lost their sparkle, and the dark circles underneath were a visual indication of her fatigue. Her shoulders drooped a little, as though she was carrying an invisible weight. Oliver couldn't help but notice the fabric of her shirt strained across her breasts, and as he glanced down her body, it seemed like she'd grown even curvier since he'd last seen her. His hands itched to touch her, to cup and caress and squeeze in all the right places.

But as he met her eyes again, he knew that wasn't going to happen.

"You're back."

There was a note of surprise in her voice, but she didn't sound especially pleased to see him. He saw the corners of her mouth dip slightly, a clear sign that she wasn't nearly as excited about this reunion as he was.

So much for a pleasurable evening. Disappointment welled in his chest, but he tried to quash the feeling. Her chilly reaction was understandable, given the fact he hadn't called since their night together. He hadn't meant to be an ass, but Hilary had no way of knowing his silence had been due to his schedule and not a lack of regard for her.

Time to do some damage control. She might not be willing to pick up where they had left off, but he didn't want her thinking the worst of him.

"I should have called."

Hilary lifted one eyebrow and tilted her head to the side. "What would you have said?"

She sounded genuinely curious. The question caught him off guard. What *would* he have said to her? *Thanks for the great night. Hope you're doing well. Let's get together again the next time I'm in town?* The words were nothing more than superficial pleasantries that did nothing to convey how she'd actually affected him. But maybe the gesture would have made a difference. Maybe it would have given him something to build on, a way to keep the door open for further communication.

He'd been so wrapped up in his project he hadn't stopped to think that for Hilary, some message from him might have been better than nothing at all.

"I don't know," he admitted. "What I can say is that I enjoyed our time together, and I hope you did, too."

Something flashed in her eyes. "You know I did," she said softly.

Masculine pleasure bloomed in his chest at her admission. "I'm glad," he replied. "I wasn't trying to ghost you," he continued. "I just got so wrapped up in my project that—"

"It's fine." She lifted her hand, cutting him off. "I knew the deal when I agreed to go out with you."

Oliver frowned. "What do you mean?"

Hilary smiled, but the expression was brittle, not happy. "Your lifestyle is no secret to me. You're always jetting off somewhere on business. I know you're not looking for anything long-term. I didn't expect anything more from you."

She was right, but for some reason, hearing her say the words stung. "Hilary, I—"

"What can I bring you to eat tonight?" She clearly wasn't in the mood for his apology or explanation. "We're pretty busy, and I have other tables."

He wanted to keep talking, to try to make her understand that he wasn't some shallow playboy who left behind a string of broken hearts. But the set of her jaw told him she wasn't interested in hearing what he had to say.

"Chicken marsala, please," he said. "And a glass of the house merlot."

He passed over his menu, wishing he could find the words to make her stay. If he could just get her to listen, he could do a better job of explaining things and she'd know that he wasn't a bad guy.

He had no choice but to watch her walk away, feeling like a window of opportunity was closing as the distance between them grew. Hilary wasn't going to give him a chance to make things right between them. It seemed unfair, but he couldn't force her to listen. And while he hated that she seemed to think so little of him, the loss of Hilary as a lover wasn't the worst part.

It was the fact that he'd lost her as a friend that bothered him the most.

Hilary stepped into the walk-in cooler and hugged herself, needing a few minutes alone to regain her composure.

Oliver Colton was back.

Logically, she'd known he would eventually return to Blue Larkspur. His family was here, and he made it a point to show up a couple of times a year to check in on them and attend any major family events. It made sense that he'd be here again, and yet his appearance still threw her.

Of course he was as handsome as ever. She'd somehow forgotten how gorgeous his eyes were. The pale blue color captured her, making her feel like she was caught under a spell. And that smile! Her skin tingled at the memory, the boyish charm in the flash of his white teeth and dimples winking from his lightly stubbled cheeks.

It was a heady thing to be the focus of Oliver's attention, to have such a handsome man express interest in her. For a few seconds, Hilary had almost felt like her old self again.

The night she'd spent with Oliver had turned out to be a sort of line in the sand. She hadn't known it at the time, but their date had turned out to be the high point of her year. Ever since she'd slept with him, her life had grown increasingly stressful. Between working on her degree and working at the restaurant, she hadn't had any time to rest and simply breathe. She was tired all the time, exhausted on a soul-deep level that no amount of sleep could touch. And on top of everything else, something was going on with her brother. Jeff was normally easygoing and friendly, but over the past few weeks he'd been short-tempered and preoccupied. Hilary had tried to talk to him, wanting to help him in some way, but he'd rebuffed all her attempts at conversation.

"I'm fine" was his gruff standard response.

At least she'd had that amazing night with Oliver.

Hilary had revisited the memories many times over the past few months, taking them out and going over them carefully whenever she felt too sorry for herself. Things might be hard now, but she had thoughts of Oliver Colton to keep her warm at night.

Seeing him now had been a jolt to her system. For a few seconds, the months of silence had disappeared. She'd wanted nothing more than to climb onto his lap and lay her head against his broad chest, to feel his strong arms circle around her as his scent filled her nose. He represented a time in her life when things had seemed easier, and she wanted so badly to go back there with him.

But that was impossible.

Maybe she should have given him a chance to explain why he hadn't called. But truth be told, it didn't matter. She'd understood their night together was a one-time experience. They'd parted on good terms—he'd had the decency to wake her the next morning to say goodbye rather than sneak off to the airport while she slept. Even though she'd known better, a small part of her had held out hope that he'd contact her again. His radio silence had stung a bit, but really, she hadn't been surprised.

Why had he come to see her again? If he was hoping for a repeat, it wasn't going to happen. Not only was she too tired to enjoy a good time, she'd gained a few pounds over the last few months and the thought of getting naked in front of Oliver was enough to make her palms sweat. Better for them to leave the past in the past. If they tried to recapture the magic again, it would likely only disappoint them both.

Besides, one dose of Oliver was all she could handle. She'd protected her heart well enough the first time around. Now that stress and fatigue had weakened her defenses, a second encounter would leave her wanting more than what he was willing to offer.

The door to the cooler jerked open and Jeff walked in, stopping short when he saw her. "What are you doing in here?"

"Just taking a moment to myself," Hilary replied.

He frowned. "Are you done? Because we're getting slammed out here and it would be nice if you would start delivering orders."

Hilary sighed. "Okay. You don't have to be a jerk about it, you know."

Jeff leveled her with a glare. "You're the one hiding in the cold room while I'm busting my ass and somehow I'm the jerk?"

"I'm not a machine," she retorted. "I'm allowed to take a break every once in a while."

Jeff snorted. "What's got you in such a bad mood? I figured you'd be happy since your boyfriend is back."

Hilary went still. "What's that supposed to mean?"

Her brother tilted his head to the side and smirked. "You think I don't know what's going on in the front of the house? I saw Oliver Colton out there, sitting in your section." He leaned closer, a malicious glint in his eyes. "You sure you're not here to steal a couple of slices of cake?"

Hilary's body went hot with anger, her skin flushing despite the cold air. "What is your problem?" she practically hissed. "You've been a real piece of work lately. You know why we're so busy? It's because we're short-staffed. And that's your fault."

Jeff reared back as though she'd slapped him. "No, it's not."

She nodded in the face of his denial. "Yeah, it is. Stacey and Jess quit because of your attitude. And I know of a couple of others who are on the verge of leaving because of the way you've been treating people. No one wants to work with a bully."

Hilary moved past her sibling, ignoring his protests. She paused at the heavy, insulated door. "You'd better rethink your attitude, before we lose even more people. Mom and Dad cut you a lot of slack, but their patience will only last so long." She shoved open the door and walked into the kitchen, leaving Jeff alone in the cold room.

Pushing thoughts of Oliver out of her mind, she focused on delivering orders and refilling drinks. But she couldn't ignore him for long—his food was up, and she couldn't very well pretend like he wasn't there.

He thanked her politely when she placed the plate in front of him. She could tell by the look on his face that he wanted to say more, but he held his tongue. Part of her was curious to know what he was thinking. But did it really matter? No amount of pretty words would change the fact that she didn't want anything from him.

She kept an eye on him from afar while he ate. Hilary told herself she was just being a good waitress, checking to make sure he didn't need anything. But she also couldn't help but look at him. Oliver had always had that effect on her—if he was around, she knew it. There was just something about him that captured her attention, like he was a radio frequency her body tuned into automatically. In the past, his presence would have made her feel hyperaware, excited, even. Now it simply added to her exhaustion.

Oliver didn't rush, but he didn't linger over his meal either. Hilary brought his check, not even bothering to ask if he wanted dessert. It was a little rude of her to effectively shoo him out of the restaurant, but she was past the point of caring about such niceties.

He signaled for her to wait as he retrieved his wallet. "I know it's been a while, but I'll be in town for a few days. Do you think we could meet and talk?" He pulled out some cash and slipped the bills inside the small folder containing his check, then handed it to her. "No change," he said softly.

Hilary hesitated, feeling torn. Oliver had just given her a very big tip. And talking sounded okay, as long as he knew it wouldn't lead to anything else. Would it be so bad to clear the air between them and part on good terms?

Before she could respond, her mother walked over. "Honey, I'm sorry to interrupt, but table seven is waiting for fresh bread, and table nine needs another glass of wine." Cheryl Weston smiled at Oliver. "It's good to see you again, Mr. Colton."

He smiled back. "You, too, Mrs. Weston. The food is as good as ever."

"I'm glad to hear it. I'll pass your compliments on to my son." Cheryl patted Hilary's shoulder and walked away.

"I have to go," Hilary said. "Enjoy your time in town."

"Wait." Oliver reached out and placed his hand on her wrist, the light touch holding her in place. A tingle shot up her arm, a visceral reminder of the connection she'd felt with him that night. "Can we talk, please?"

Hilary shook her head and stepped back, cutting the physical connection between them. "There's no need," she replied. "I've already moved on."

Oliver frowned. "You're seeing someone?"

Hilary nodded, happy for him to make that assumption. "Uh, yes. I am." Never mind that the only people she saw these days were her coworkers, and the only male attention she received were the "thank yous" she got for delivering food and drinks to a table. If Oliver thinking she had a boyfriend was the key to ending this awkward moment, she'd roll with it.

He nodded slowly. "He's a lucky guy," he said, almost to himself.

She took another step back as he got to his feet. She'd forgotten how tall he was, how much space he took up with his broad shoulders and long legs. He stared down at her, his blue eyes full of an emotion she couldn't identify. For a split second, it looked like he wanted to kiss her. But surely that was just a trick of the light?

"Take care of yourself, Hilary." His smile was warm, but it didn't quite reach his eyes. She thought she detected a hint of regret in his voice. Uneasiness shot through her; what if she was making a mistake?

Before she could debate any further, Oliver slipped past her. He was careful to keep their bodies from touching as he walked by, but she felt a trace of his heat all the same. She sucked in a breath, catching a note of his scent. Her legs went wobbly as the memories she'd been working hard to suppress rushed to the forefront of her mind—Oliver's weight settling over her, his mouth trailing down her neck, the rasp of his stubble on her thighs as he explored her intimate places. It was enough to make her want to run after him and beg for a repeat of that night, consequences be damned.

She took a half step in his direction, as if pulled by a magnetic force. But before she could move again, her mother caught her eye. Cheryl angled her head meaningfully in the direction of Hilary's tables, a silent reminder to get back to work. Hilary sighed and nodded slightly in acknowledgment.

Oliver Colton was charming, sexy and completely out of reach. Their lifestyles couldn't have been more different. And while his surprise reappearance had made her briefly wish for something more, Hilary knew that her reality wasn't going to change. She needed to shake off his effects and get back to work. Daydreaming about things that weren't going to happen was simply a waste of time and energy, and she was already short on both these days.

With that in mind, Hilary took a deep breath and pasted on a smile. She headed for her closest table. "How is everything tonight?" she said quietly. "May I bring you another glass of wine?"

What am I doing?

It wasn't the first time he'd asked himself that question this evening, but Oliver still didn't have a good answer. At this hour, he should be in his hotel room, relaxing with a book or watching a little television before going to bed. So why was he driving aimlessly in his rental car, traveling the familiar streets of Blue Larkspur without really seeing anything?

Hilary wasn't the one for him. He knew this— their lives were far too different. She was a staple of Blue Larkspur; her job was here, her family and friends. She had roots in this town. Whereas he was constantly on the go. Sure, he returned to see his family when he could, but his daily life was a series of flights and phone calls, meetings and fundraisers to drum up capital for his latest projects. He was never in one place for very long, and for the most part, he liked it that way.

Aside from their lifestyle differences, there was also the fact that Hilary had a boyfriend now. It wasn't surprising—she was an attractive woman with a great sense of humor. Of course she wasn't going to stay single just so they could continue to hook up each time he was in town. She'd moved on, and while he didn't enjoy the thought of her with another man, he understood.

So why was he still thinking about her, hours after seeing her again? He'd never had a problem putting an unavailable woman out of his mind before. What made Hilary so different? Why did this particular rejection sting so much?

He stopped for a red light and glanced around, taking stock of his surroundings. Atria was on the corner, the parking lot empty save for a couple of cars. He recognized Hilary's vehicle and realized she was still inside, likely helping close up the place for the night.

Before he knew what he was doing, Oliver turned right and maneuvered into the parking lot. Even though Blue Larkspur was a relatively safe community, he didn't like the idea of Hilary walking to her car alone.

He parked next to her, wondering if he was crossing a line somehow. Hilary had made it clear there was nothing between them. He accepted that, but still... They'd shared more than an amazing night together. Oliver had always considered her a friend. Was it possible they could still hold on to that aspect of their relationship? Or did she want nothing to do with him at all?

He hadn't gotten the chance to ask her earlier. Her mother had stopped by, making it clear Hilary shouldn't linger with him. Did Mrs. Weston know about their rendezvous? Perhaps she thought he was bad news and wanted to keep her daughter away from him.

But he'd seen a glimmer of regret in Hilary's eyes as the older woman had walked away. He could have sworn there was more Hilary had wanted to say to him, and he definitely had some things he wanted to discuss with her. So he'd catch her after work, when she didn't have the distraction of customers waiting for their food or drink refills. Maybe now that it was just the two of them, they could really talk things over.

And if she still wanted nothing to do with him? Then he'd wish her well and leave her alone. He wasn't going to force himself into her life. He would miss her, but he would respect her decision.

Oliver rolled down the windows and cut the engine. A warm breeze drifted through the interior of the car, ruffling his hair a bit. The evening was quiet, save for the sounds of passing cars on the nearby road.

He glanced at his watch. How long did it take to

close up this place? The wind picked up, sending a strong gust through the car. Movement from the restaurant caught his attention, and he turned to see the front door of Atria open a bit, then stop as if meeting some kind of resistance from inside.

Oliver frowned at the sight, a sense of uneasiness building in his chest. The restaurant was closed so that door should be locked, not flapping in the wind. The most logical explanation was that someone had forgotten to fully close it after the last customers had left. So why did his imagination immediately conjure up thoughts of a robbery?

Too many crime shows, he thought as he shook his head. He was a sucker for those cold case stories and murder investigation docuseries, which was ironic given his father's crimes. Part of it was his brother Gavin's fault; Oliver had started listening to his true crime podcast as a gesture of support and had quickly gotten hooked. He should probably switch to some lighter content. He decided to stop immediately jumping to the wrong conclusion when faced with an innocuous situation.

Still, he couldn't just leave the door swinging open like that. Even though he seemed to be the only person around, it wasn't safe.

Oliver climbed out of the car and walked across the parking lot to the entrance. Another surge of wind pushed the door in as he approached, and he saw the place was dark inside. "Hello?" he called out as he stood at the threshold. "Hilary? Are you still in there?"

There was no response. The hairs on the back of his neck stood at attention as the door thumped against something heavy. Had the umbrella stand fallen over to block the entrance? Hilary wasn't the type to leave things out of order—she must not have noticed it yet.

Oliver decided to step inside so he could find her. She had to be about to finish the closing process by now.

"Hilary?" He pushed gently against the door, raising his voice to just below a yell. She was probably in the kitchen in the back and couldn't hear him.

The door met resistance again. Oliver pushed a little harder, but whatever was blocking the way was solid and didn't move willingly.

He put some force behind his push and was able to step inside. There was definitely something on the floor, but it wasn't the umbrella stand.

Oliver blinked, his eyes adjusting quickly to the darkness. A dark, solid mass was heaped on the tile floor. At first, he thought it was a bundle of coats. But it was too solid, and no one was wearing heavy layers in August.

His heart dropped to his stomach and a chill rushed through his body as he finally recognized what he was seeing.

A body.

Oliver dropped to his knees, his hands shaking as he reached out to touch the person. Were they dead?

Please, no…

Time seemed to slow to a crawl as his hand closed the distance between them. While he moved, he became aware of other details that he hadn't initially noticed.

White shirt.

Black pants.

Blond hair.

No, it can't be.

Like a scene from a nightmare, Oliver placed his hand on the person's shoulder and rolled them to their back, exposing their face. His heart stuttered in his chest as he learned the answer to the question he hadn't dared to ask.

It was Hilary.

Chapter 3

"Hilary!"

Oliver's voice sounded strange to his own ears as he repeated her name, his anxiety building with every second she didn't respond.

He put his hands on her shoulders and shook a bit, hoping to rouse her. "Please wake up!"

What had happened here? Was she hurt? Or had she simply passed out while locking up?

There was no visible blood on her clothes, but would he even see the stains on her black pants in the darkness? Oliver ran his hands over her body, searching for wetness or warmth. He breathed out a shaky sigh when he encountered neither.

He had to call for help. Whatever had happened

here, Hilary needed medical attention. He yelled for help—surely she hadn't been closing up by herself?

Silence met his cries.

If someone had been here, they were gone now. He debated getting up to search the place, but quickly dismissed the thought. No way was he going to leave her side, not when she was like this.

Moving quickly, Oliver tugged his phone from his pocket and punched in 9-1-1. The dispatcher answered in a few rings, and he described the situation, his eyes never leaving Hilary's face as he spoke.

"Please hurry," he said, unable to hide the note of panic in his voice. She was so still. Why wasn't she moving? Would she wake up?

Oliver wanted to touch her, but he didn't know if that would make things worse.

"Is she responding?" asked the dispatcher.

"No. Should I try to wake her?"

"Take your knuckles and rub them over her heart. You'll need to press a bit."

Oliver frowned. "Won't that hurt?"

"That's the idea."

He hesitated a second, then did as he was told. "I'm sorry," he muttered, apologizing even though he doubted Hilary could hear him.

He pressed his knuckles into her skin and moved them up and down her breastbone. She grimaced and tried to move away.

"She's responding!" A burst of relief spread through

him and he barely resisted the temptation to pull her into his arms.

"That's good." The dispatcher's voice was simultaneously soothing and encouraging. "Try talking to her."

Oliver didn't have to be told twice. "Hilary, can you wake up? Come on, I need you to open your eyes for me." He kept babbling, forcing the words past the lump in his throat. She had to be okay—he couldn't entertain any other possibilities.

She moaned, the sound small and afraid. His heart thumped hard against his ribs, the desire to help her, to do *something* to fix this situation, warring with the reality that there was nothing more he *could* do.

He kept talking, trying to pull her out of whatever darkness she was in. Gradually, he became aware of the sound of sirens in the background. Still, he kept his focus on Hilary. She looked so helpless, so innocent. What the hell had happened here?

Something landed on his shoulder and he jumped at the unexpected contact. He glanced up to see the EMTs had arrived.

"You did great," the young man said, looking down at him with a kind expression. "Let us take over, okay?"

Oliver nodded and scooted back to allow the men better access. He hated letting go of Hilary's hand, but he had to let the professionals do their job.

There were two of them, one kneeling on either side of her. They talked to each other as they worked, the voices a low murmur, speaking in an easy short-hand Oliver couldn't understand.

"Sir? Sir?"

The voice was coming from his phone. Oliver stared at the device he was holding, trying to recall who he'd been speaking to.

He lifted it to his ear. "Hello?"

"It sounds like the ambulance has arrived. I'm going to disconnect the call now."

Awareness dawned. The dispatcher. Of course. "Yes, thank you," he replied automatically. He slipped the phone into his pocket and sat on the floor, staring at Hilary and the paramedics but not really seeing anything.

His brain simply couldn't comprehend what was going on. He'd spoken to her just a few hours ago. She'd seemed tired and uncharacteristically down, but otherwise normal. So why was she now lying unconscious on the floor of the restaurant? Had she gone to lock the door and passed out? Or had something more sinister happened?

And why was she alone? No one had responded to his earlier calls for help. He hadn't done a search of the place, but he'd bet no one had been here for a while.

Anger bloomed in his chest. Hilary shouldn't have been by herself, especially at night. Someone should have been working with her to close the restaurant. Wasn't that standard procedure?

There was movement at the door again. The police this time. He watched as one officer and then a second slipped through the gap and entered, stepping around the EMTs and Hilary. One of them knelt and spoke in a low voice, while the other glanced around, assessing the situation.

He caught sight of Oliver and walked over. "What's your name, sir?"

Oliver managed to get to his feet though his knees felt a bit wobbly. "Oliver Colton," he replied. From this vantage point he could see Hilary's face. Her eyes appeared to be open, but she was squinting so he couldn't be sure.

"You're the one who found her?"

He tore his gaze from Hilary and focused on the man in front of him. The cop was about his height, his salt-and-pepper hair cropped close in a military-style cut. There were frown lines at the corners of his brown eyes, and he looked like a man who had seen things.

"Yes, she was on the ground when I arrived. Officer…?" He trailed off, waiting for the man to introduce himself.

"Simpkins," the man replied. Oliver made a mental note to have his mom ask Chief Lawson about this guy. Since Lawson was sweet on her, he'd probably be happy to tell her if Simpkins was a good cop. He wanted only the best, because if his suspicions were correct and someone had deliberately hurt Hilary, Oliver wanted them found and arrested as soon as possible.

"Walk me through what happened tonight."

Oliver told him everything he knew, starting from when he noticed the door was open to finding Hilary and calling 9-1-1. Officer Simpkins listened carefully, nodding here and there until Oliver finished.

"Why did you come back to the restaurant?"

Oliver frowned. "I told you, I needed to talk to Hilary."

"Why not wait until tomorrow?"

A bubble of frustration rose in Oliver's chest. "I don't know her work schedule. I wanted to speak with her tonight."

"I see." Just two words, but they contained a world of skepticism.

Oliver sighed. "What are you implying, Officer? That I assaulted Hilary and then called the police?"

Simpkins shrugged. "Stranger things have happened."

"Maybe so, but that's not what happened here." A kernel of worry began to grow in his stomach. Did this man really think Oliver had hurt Hilary? Was he going to arrest him on suspicion of assault? "Should I call my lawyer?" Three of his siblings were attorneys; at least one of them would be able to help him in a pinch like this.

Simpkins raised one eyebrow at the question. "Have you done anything to warrant the need for counsel?"

Oliver tilted his head to the side. "No. But my sister, the district attorney, has always told me not to talk to the police without her." It was a lesson he'd learned the hard way. He hadn't always been a model citizen; in fact, many in town had called him a teenage delinquent. He'd spent a lot of time drinking and partying after his father's death, and he'd found himself sleeping things off in a holding cell on more than one occasion. Fortunately, his legal troubles hadn't been of the prison sentence variety. Even more importantly, Ezra and Dom hadn't given up on him, and they'd helped him turn things around before he made the kind of mistake that couldn't be forgiven.

Officer Simpkins narrowed his eyes at the mention of Rachel. "I wondered if there was a connection," he muttered, seemingly to himself.

Looking over the man's shoulder, Oliver noticed the paramedics had transferred Hilary to a gurney and appeared to be preparing to move her. "Excuse me," he said, moving past to draw closer to her.

"Now wait a minute—" Simpkins protested, but Oliver didn't pay attention to him. He was totally focused on Hilary. She was awake now, her features drawn in a grimace of pain.

"Hilary?" He stood by her head, looking down at her.

"Oliver?" She squinted up at him, still frowning. "Is that you?"

"Yes, I'm here." Relief flooded through him at the sound of her voice. It was hard to see her like this, shaken and fragile. But the fact that she'd recognized his voice was a good sign.

"What happened? What are you doing here?"

"I don't know," he admitted. "I came back to talk to you and found you on the ground."

"Ma'am, we need to go," said one of the paramedics.

They started to roll her away but she grew agitated. "Wait! Oliver, stay with me!"

He didn't have to be told twice. He trotted after them as they wheeled her through the door and into the parking lot.

Officer Simpkins followed, close on his heels. "I'm not done talking to you, Mr. Colton."

Oliver spared him a glance. "I don't know what else I can tell you, but I'm not going anywhere. If it really can't wait until tomorrow, you can find me at the hospital with her."

Simpkins frowned, clearly unhappy with Oliver's declaration. "I will be contacting you," he said. Given his tone, Oliver couldn't tell if it was a promise or a threat. "I need to finish taking your statement."

Oliver paused while the paramedics lifted the gurney into the back of the ambulance. "Look, Officer, I want the same thing as you here. To find out who hurt Hilary and make sure they answer for it. You probably hear this all the time, but I am not your guy. Please don't waste your time blaming me when you could be finding the people who are responsible."

Simpkins studied him for a second, as if trying to gauge his sincerity. "I'm only letting you go now because she's asked for you. I will be seeing you at the hospital after my partner and I finish up here."

"Thank you." It grated on Oliver's nerves to act grateful when the truth was, he had no intention of staying behind while Hilary was taken away. But he didn't want to needlessly antagonize the police and cause them to suspect him of something he hadn't done.

"Oliver?" Hilary's voice drifted from the back of the ambulance. The plaintive sound pulled at him, drawing him away from Simpkins. Oliver stepped over to stand at the back of the ambulance, wanting to jump on board but uncertain as to the etiquette of the situation. He didn't want to take up too much room or get in the way of the paramedics, but the thought of leaving Hilary alone back there was unacceptable.

The man who'd spoken to him earlier caught sight of him. "Yeah, all right," he said, gesturing for Oliver to climb inside. "You can sit there."

Oliver slid onto the bench and reached for Hilary's hand. "I'm here," he told her. "It's going to be okay."

Hilary briefly closed her eyes, appearing to relax for the first time since he'd found her on the floor. "Yeah," she breathed. "If you say so."

The paramedic shut the back doors and tapped against the small window that looked into the driver's section. At the signal, the ambulance began rolling forward.

Oliver shifted to remain balanced on his seat. As

the vehicle picked up speed, Hilary grimaced and moaned slightly.

"What's wrong?" he asked. He glanced at the paramedic, seeking reassurance.

"My stomach," she said. "The movement is making me nauseated."

"You're okay," said the EMT. He fished out a small square package from a nearby bag and ripped open the wrapper. The scent of rubbing alcohol hit Oliver's nose as the young man reached over to hold the packet close to Hilary's face. "This should help."

Hilary sniffed delicately. After a moment, her features eased and her face lost the pinched look of distress.

Oliver felt himself relax as well. It was strange, feeling this attuned to her. Of course he cared about her, but he'd never imagined his worry and concern would put knots in his stomach and make his shoulders so tense.

"We're almost there," he said, half to Hilary and half to himself. Once they got to the hospital and the doctors examined her, they'd know more about what had happened to her and hopefully get reassurance about her condition.

Questions swirled through his brain one after the other, forming a tangled mess of thoughts. But as he looked at Hilary on the gurney, holding her hand through the jostles and bumps of the journey to the hospital, he took some comfort from the fact that right now, she appeared to be okay.

This definitely wasn't how he'd expected the night to end. Still, part of him was glad he'd been the one to find her. If he hadn't come along, who knows how long she would have lain there alone on the floor?

Oliver pushed the disturbing thought aside and squeezed Hilary's hand. She turned her head to look at him, and he mustered up a smile.

"Thank you," she said softly.

Oliver's eyes stung and his throat tightened with emotion. He didn't deserve her gratitude when all he'd done was call for help.

Not knowing what to say, he leaned forward and pressed a kiss to the back of her hand. "I'm here," he replied. "It's going to be okay."

And it would. He'd do everything in his power to make sure of it.

Hilary couldn't keep her eyes open. The pain in her head throbbed with every beat of her heart, marking the passage of time in a hideous fashion. If she moved, the agony increased. Lights made it worse. Even sound was torture. She wanted nothing more than to lie in a dark, quiet room, alone and unbothered so she could get some kind of control over the pounding in her head.

The emergency room was the complete opposite of what she needed.

Bright overhead lights speared her eyes, stabbing like toothpicks. Something was beeping in the background—the sound had been there when she'd arrived, however long ago that was now, and it gave no sign of stopping. And the scent—*ugh!* That smell of bleach and cleanser hung in the air, turning her stomach and making the bile rise up the back of her throat.

The experience was a sensory overload.

At least they were leaving her alone for the moment. When the ambulance had first arrived, there had been a hum of activity around her. Nurses and doctors examining her, moving her, ordering tests. She'd been poked and prodded, asked a lot of questions that she'd struggled to answer. They'd done some kind of imaging on her head, and she'd had to lie on her face while someone stitched a gash on the base of her skull. She'd been overwhelmed by it all, but she hadn't been able to say so in the face of everything that was happening.

"It's okay." A low, calm voice spoke nearby.

Oliver.

He was still here.

She'd appreciated his presence during the ambulance ride. The feel of his hand wrapped around hers had grounded her, given her something to focus on to distract from the discomfort of being moved. But now that they'd reached the hospital and the doctors had done their preliminary exams, she was a little surprised that he was still with her.

Her parents hadn't made it to the hospital yet—she imagined they were still talking to the police and dealing with the aftermath of the situation at the restaurant. In a strange way, she was glad for their absence. She didn't think she could handle her mother's emotions right now, not with everything else going on.

Moving carefully, she turned her head to the side and cracked open her eyes to see him. He was sitting in a chair next to her bed, his elbows resting on his knees as he leaned forward. His hair was mussed, as though he'd been running his hands through it.

"You look tired," she said. "You should go get some rest."

It was the truth, though her motives weren't purely altruistic. The idea that Oliver Colton was here, seeing her at her worst, made her uncomfortable. Hilary didn't think of herself as being particularly vain, but she did have standards for herself. And right now, there was no way she looked good. Bad enough she was dealing with the worst headache of all time; knowing Oliver was here to witness it made things just a little bit worse.

He met her eyes, his blue gaze steady. "Do you want me to go?"

It was a simple question, but for the life of her, Hilary couldn't bring herself to say yes. Even though she hated feeling vulnerable in front of him, the idea of being here alone was frightening. At this point, she was in too much pain to understand much of what the doctors might tell her. It would be nice to have someone here, at least until her family arrived.

A soft knock stalled her response. Hilary closed her eyes again as she heard the door open.

"Hi there." It was the voice of her nurse, a sweet young woman who had introduced herself earlier. The problem was, Hilary couldn't remember her name at the moment.

"The doctor said you can have something for your pain now," the nurse continued.

Hilary bit her tongue to keep from crying out in relief. At last!

"I'll just get this ready and you should be feeling better soon." Hilary heard the sounds of typing and a quiet beep as something was scanned. Then she felt movement at her side.

"Can you confirm your name and birthday for me?"

Hilary responded, then said, "What are you giving me?" She didn't know anything about medication, but it seemed like an important question to ask.

"This is morphine," the nurse replied. "I'm just going to inject it through your IV. It will start to work very quickly."

Relief couldn't come soon enough. Hilary wasn't sure how much longer she could tolerate this headache.

She didn't know how long it took the nurse to administer the drug. But she felt it take hold of her.

The pounding in her head began to dull, as though someone had turned the volume down. The muscles she hadn't realized were tense began to relax, and she felt herself settle onto the bed. Even though her eyes were closed, things started to feel hazy and buoyant, like she was floating on cotton candy clouds.

She dimly heard the door again but couldn't figure out if someone was coming or going.

"Do you want me to leave?"

Oliver's words floated around her, so close she could reach out and touch them.

She must have lifted her hand to do that, because she felt the warmth of his touch against her palm. That was nice.

Wait. Had he asked a question?

She tried to organize her thoughts. But before she could muster a response, she slipped under the surface of consciousness, embracing the dark relief that waited for her.

Chapter 4

Oliver shifted on the small sofa in Hilary's room. One of the nurses had brought him a pillow and blanket a few hours ago, but he hadn't been able to sleep. Despite the time, people had been coming and going as though this was an airport, not a hospital.

Hilary's parents had arrived soon after she'd managed to fall asleep. Oliver bit his tongue as they tried to wake her up, trying to put himself in their shoes. If that were his child in the bed, he'd want to speak to them and hear their voice. Hilary did rouse for a few moments, but fortunately she was able to fall asleep again quickly. To their credit, her parents didn't try to force her to stay awake.

The police had stopped by as well. Officer Simpkins had frowned when he saw that Hilary wasn't able to answer questions, but Oliver was able to finish giving his statement. The older man grudgingly acknowledged that a cursory review of the security footage at the restaurant showed two masked men enter the place shortly after closing. Oliver was relieved to hear they had some evidence to investigate. At least now he could be sure Simpkins wouldn't waste time trying to implicate him for something he hadn't done.

Hilary's parents had left after about an hour. They'd both been subdued and quiet, holding each other as they walked down the hall. They'd stopped by Oliver, standing close as he wrapped up his conversation with Officer Simpkins.

"You're the one who found her?" asked Hilary's father.

Oliver nodded. "Yes. The police told me about the masked men who entered the restaurant. I wish I had arrived sooner." Two against one wasn't great odds, but he might have been able to scare the intruders away before they hurt Hilary. At the very least, he would have put up a fight to protect her.

"Thank you for calling the ambulance," said her mother.

"They came very quickly," Oliver replied, hoping to reassure them. "The doctor said she should make a full recovery."

"That's good," said her father.

Oliver knew they were both stressed and worried

for Hilary, but he had to ask the question that had been bothering him since he'd found her. "Why was she alone tonight?"

Hilary's mother let out a little sob and turned her face to her husband's shoulder. The older man tightened his embrace and his lips thinned. "She wasn't. Her brother was supposed to be there with her."

Oliver frowned, trying to recall if he'd ever met her brother before. She'd mentioned him a few times in conversation, and Oliver knew he was the chef at the restaurant. But he'd never met the man before. Why had he left his sister to close the place by herself? Didn't he realize how dangerous that could be?

"Where was he?" Oliver knew her parents weren't to blame, but he couldn't keep the anger out of his voice.

"We don't know," said Mr. Weston. "He's missing."

Now Oliver watched Hilary sleep in the dim light of the hospital room, wondering if she realized her brother was nowhere to be found. Had he told her where he was going when he'd left her at the restaurant tonight? Perhaps he'd had a date or hadn't been feeling well. Or maybe those masked men hadn't been there for a simple robbery. It was possible Jeff was in some kind of trouble and they'd come for him. Had he caught sight of them and fled, abandoning his sister in the face of a threat? Or had the men taken him and Hilary had been injured while trying to protect her sibling?

It was the kind of thing she'd do, he mused. If she saw something happening, Hilary wouldn't think twice about stepping in to try to help a relative in need. Even if she put herself in danger in the process.

So many questions. But the only person with any answers was currently asleep, and hopefully would remain that way for a while.

Oliver stretched out his legs and crossed his ankles. At some point he would have to leave her and get some rest. But he couldn't bring himself to go while it was still dark. Even though she wasn't technically alone in the hospital, he hated the thought of her waking up here, confused and scared.

The door opened and a nurse entered, rolling a small pole with a monitor at the top. "Just doing a vitals check," she whispered. She approached the bed and began her work, moving quietly so as not to disturb Hilary. Once she was finished, she logged in to the computer in the corner and began typing.

"Do you have her OB's contact information?" she asked.

Oliver blinked, taken aback by the question. "I'm sorry, what?"

"Her obstetrician's information," the nurse clarified. "I'm sure the baby is fine, but we like to notify the OB when one of their patients has been admitted."

The baby? What on earth was the nurse talking about? He glanced at Hilary, trying to appraise her figure. She'd seemed curvier when she'd waited on him earlier that night, but surely she wasn't pregnant?

Or was she?

"Sir?"

The nurse's voice broke through his thoughts. Oliver shook his head. "Uh, no. I'm sorry, I don't know her doctor's name."

"That's okay." She finished typing and gave him a quick smile. "We can get it from her when she wakes up."

"Yeah," Oliver said blankly.

The nurse rolled her equipment out of the room and shut the door behind her. Oliver sat up, his eyes locked on Hilary's stomach as his mind raced.

There must be some kind of mistake. Hilary would have mentioned it she was pregnant. Right?

"Maybe not," he murmured. After all, she'd basically brushed him off. Why share that kind of information with someone she had no intention of seeing again?

But what if she *was* pregnant?

The baby couldn't be his, he decided immediately. They'd only been together the one time, and they'd been careful about using protection. So if she was indeed expecting, the father must be the man she was currently seeing.

Jealousy flickered to life in a corner of his heart. The fact that Hilary had not only moved on with someone else but was now having that man's child made Oliver feel a tiny bit wistful. He wasn't ready for kids right now, but he'd always thought he'd have them someday. After their amazing night together, his imagination had started casting Hilary as the part of his future wife. But after her rejection tonight, and now with the news of her pregnancy, he realized that was never going to happen.

So where was her new guy?

Oliver kicked himself for not asking her parents to contact the man. He was the one who should be with Hilary now, waiting for her to wake up.

But…she'd wanted *him* tonight. She hadn't called out for another man when the paramedics were looking after her, she'd said his name. She'd asked for him to come along to the hospital. Maybe that was because his was the only familiar face she'd seen after waking up on the floor of the restaurant. Or perhaps there was something more to it…

Hilary had told him she'd moved on with someone else. What if she'd been lying? Or what if the other guy she'd slept with was no longer in the picture? Did he even know about the baby?

Oliver's protective instincts flared to life as his imagination ran wild, conjuring up a scenario where Hilary had told this faceless stranger she was carrying his child, only to be rejected by him. The life of a single mother was hard—he'd seen the way his mother had struggled after his father had died, even though none of his siblings had been babies at the time. He hated the thought of Hilary having to take care of a newborn by herself. The sleepless nights, the feeding, the crying—she deserved a partner to help her as she embarked on this new chapter of her life.

Nervous energy filled him, making him jittery. Unable to sit still any longer, Oliver got to his feet and began to pace at the foot of her bed. Why did he feel so anxious about Hilary and her future? He had no responsibility here—this wasn't his baby and they weren't a couple. He was her former friend turned one-time lover who popped into town every few months to say hi. Given his career and his traveling schedule, what could he even do for her? And if he did find a way to help her, would she accept? She was a proud woman who had made it clear she didn't have space in her life for him. Should he even bother to try?

Yes. The answer came to him before he'd even finished asking himself the question. Even though they didn't have a romantic future together, he still considered Hilary to be a friend. She might not feel the same way about him, but he needed to at least offer his assistance. If she turned him down, he could walk away, knowing he'd tried his best.

He stopped and turn to stare down at her, his eyes drawn to her abdomen. She looked so peaceful lying there, her breathing even, her face no longer pinched with pain. The memory of waking up next to her popped into his head, and for a moment, he was back in that hotel room with her. He'd studied her face before waking her to say goodbye, tracing the lines of her features with his eyes. She'd been so beautiful. She was still beautiful, despite the changed circumstances.

He ran a hand through his hair. His head ached and his eyes burned, likely a combination of emotion and fatigue. This visit home was supposed to be a simple reunion with family and friends, a temporary stopover until he had to travel for his next business venture. Instead, things were growing more complicated by the minute.

No one would blame him for walking away. He'd done the right thing by calling the ambulance when he'd found Hilary unconscious on the floor. There was no reason he had to stay with her now.

Except he couldn't stomach the thought of leaving. Not until he knew for certain that she was going to be okay.

He shuffled back to the sofa and sat, trying to find a comfortable position. If he was going to stay, he had to try harder to get some rest. Given everything that had happened tonight, there was no telling what surprises tomorrow would bring.

One thing was certain: he had to be ready for anything.

Hilary woke slowly, swimming to the surface of consciousness with tentative strokes. She cracked open her eyes and held her breath, bracing for the onslaught of pain. But instead of the throbbing, insistent agony of last night, she felt a mild ache. The back of her head stung a bit, and she recalled the doctors stitching her scalp.

She opened her eyes fully and took stock of her surroundings. A television hung on the wall across from her bed, and there was a bathroom in the right corner. She dimly recalled seeing pieces of the room during the night, when the nurses woke her for status checks. It looked different in the light of day—less frightening, more bland and ordinary.

Fragmented memories of yesterday's events began to play in her mind. She frowned and rubbed her forehead, trying to make sense of the noises and images filling her head. She looked over at the window, hoping for something to distract her, to give her something else to focus on so she could try to organize her thoughts.

That's when she saw him.

Oliver Colton was lying on his side on the small sofa under the window, his legs drawn up and his head resting on a flat hospital pillow. The sight of him hit her like a physical blow, causing her to shift back in her bed.

What was he doing here? She remembered asking him to come with her, and she remembered him being there when the nurse had given her the morphine. But she hadn't expected him to stay overnight. There was no way that couch was comfortable, and once she'd gone to sleep there had been no reason for him to keep her company.

Warmth bloomed in her chest as she studied him,

her eyes tracing the slope of his broad shoulders and the curve of his knees. His mouth was slightly open, his face totally relaxed. A tuft of hair swept over his forehead, giving him a boyish look. Even in sleep, he was a handsome man.

She'd never seen him like this before. After their night together, he'd been the one to wake her before leaving, so she hadn't gotten a glimpse of him looking so vulnerable. Her stomach did a funny little flip at the intimacy of the scene, and she realized she was getting a peek at the man behind the curtain. Oliver was normally so strong and confident, completely at ease in his own skin and projecting a readiness that made her think he could handle anything. Now, though, she could almost see the boy he'd once been. A sense of tenderness washed over her; if she'd been close enough to touch him, she would have reached out and brushed the hair off his forehead.

It was probably for the best that she couldn't.

As much as she was attracted to him, Oliver wasn't the man for her. She'd told him as much last night, and he'd seemed to accept that.

So why was he still here?

As if sensing her gaze, he blinked a few times and opened his eyes. Their eyes locked, and he gave her a soft smile. "Hey."

"Hey, yourself," she replied. "I'm surprised you're still here."

He grimaced slightly and stretched, his body unfolding as he sat up. The fabric of his shirt shifted, revealing a tantalizing glimpse of his flat stomach. Hilary forced herself to look away. The last thing she needed was a reminder of his physical attributes, especially since there was no way she'd ever get to enjoy them again.

Oliver grunted slightly. "Doing okay?" she asked.

"Yeah," he said. "Just feeling my age this morning."

"You can't have gotten much sleep last night."

"I didn't," he confirmed. "But that's okay."

She glanced back at him, deciding to press for an answer to her question. "I don't mean to sound ungrateful, but why did you stay? I appreciate you coming to the hospital with me, but I never meant to make you feel obligated to spend the night here."

"You didn't," he said shortly. "I just wanted to make sure someone was here with you. In case you woke up scared, or something happened."

Hilary sat with his response for a moment, trying to decide how to feel about his answer. On the one hand, she was touched by his concern. The fact that he'd stuck by her side, despite his own discomfort, made her feel cared for and important. But on the other hand, his presence bothered her a little. She was trying to get over him, to move past her feelings and desire for him. Having him so close, being the recipient of his thoughtfulness, made the process a lot more difficult.

"Thank you," she said finally. There was no point in arguing with him about what he should or shouldn't have done—the night was over, and he was still here. She didn't owe him anything more than gratitude for his presence, and Oliver didn't appear to have expectations of more.

"Do you remember what happened last night?" His tone was casual, but there was an intensity in his eyes that made it clear Oliver was hoping she had information to share.

Hilary closed her eyes briefly. "Yeah," she said, sighing as the memories returned. "I do."

"The police want to talk to you. Do you feel up to speaking with them? I know you just woke up, so if you need some time, it's okay."

"No, let's get it over with." The sooner she spoke to them, the better. Her brother's face flashed in her mind, the memory accompanied by a stab of fear. Something terrible had happened last night, and she wanted answers.

Oliver got to his feet and walked to the far corner of the room, retrieving his phone from his pocket as he walked. She heard him talking softly and figured he was calling the police. Hilary focused on her breathing, pushing down her worries for Jeff. Hopefully, her brother was fine. But if that was the case, why wasn't he here?

Oliver returned to the sofa and sat with a sigh. "The officers will be here in about fifteen minutes. They're eager to hear what you have to say."

"I have some questions for them as well." She leaned back against the pillow and bit her bottom lip.

Oliver probably didn't know anything, but it wouldn't hurt to ask. "Do you…" She trailed off, then tried again. "Have you heard anything about Jeff?"

Oliver's expression softened. "I haven't," he said gently. "I'm sorry."

Tears stung her eyes, and she shook her head. "That's okay," she said. "Hopefully the police will know something."

"Do you want me to call your parents? Or…anyone else?" he added delicately.

"No," she said immediately. She remembered seeing her mom and dad last night, so she knew they were okay. But the thought of facing her folks right now was overwhelming. She'd reach out to them later, after she'd given her statement to the police and spoken to her doctor.

Oliver gave her a quizzical look but didn't reply beyond a nod.

Hilary shifted on the bed. There was one thing that was bothering her, and she knew Oliver was the only person with an answer.

"So why did you come back to Atria last night?"

He raised one eyebrow and she rushed to continue. "I mean, I'm glad you did. If you hadn't found me, I don't know what would have happened." She shuddered to think of the possibilities— would she have woken up eventually, in pain and disoriented? Or would her mother have found her when she'd come to open the restaurant in the morning? Either way,

Oliver's appearance had been a lucky stroke that had kept things from getting worse.

"Are you asking why I returned after you'd given me the brush-off?"

Hilary frowned, not appreciating his description of their conversation. She hadn't ignored him or dismissed him out of hand. She'd simply acted to protect her heart.

But squabbling over semantics wasn't going to get her anywhere. So she swallowed her defensive retort and settled for a nod. "Something like that."

Oliver glanced away and ran a hand through his hair. He let out a sigh that told her he didn't want to answer her question, but after a few seconds of silence, he spoke.

"The truth is, I wanted to talk to you. I didn't like the way things ended between us at the restaurant."

Hilary's heart started to beat hard as she considered his words. Was Oliver trying to tell her that he didn't want to let her go? That he wanted to have a real relationship with her, rather than a "friends with benefits" arrangement whenever he happened to be in town?

"I see," she said, trying to keep any trace of hope or excitement out of her voice. Could they make something work, given his near constant traveling? Or did he mean for her to go with him? For a brief instant, she imagined herself traveling the world on Oliver's arm, visiting new cities and countries as he jetted around on business. She could even continue to earn her degree, since her program was online. What would that be like, to enter his world?

"It felt like you were closing a door on me," he continued. "And while I have no intention of pressuring you into changing your mind about a physical relationship with me, I do want us to remain friends."

"Friends," she echoed weakly.

And just like that, her fantasy of a relationship with Oliver Colton died a quick death.

He nodded, looking almost earnest. "Of course," she heard herself say. "We can still be friends."

"I'm glad to hear it," he said. "Because I do still care about you." He placed his hand over hers, his touch warm. But now that she knew he had no romantic interest in her, she took no comfort from the gesture.

Really, though, could she blame him? Wasn't this the outcome she'd hoped for when she'd seen him at the restaurant last night? Hilary had told him she wasn't up for something casual, had implied she'd moved on with someone else, and he'd taken her words to heart.

So why did that leave her feeling a bit hollow inside?

"I'm glad that's settled," she said, trying to regain her equilibrium.

"Me, too," he replied. "Especially because I think you could really use your friends now."

Hilary frowned, wondering what he meant by that. It was an uncharacteristically cryptic remark for him—from the time they'd spent together, Oliver didn't strike her as the kind of man who had trouble saying what he was thinking.

Before she could ask him to clarify, there was a knock at the door and two police officers entered. Oliver clearly recognized the two men, and he shook their hands like they were all old friends. Apparently, his charming nature wasn't only effective against females.

The cops approached her and introduced themselves. They had been the ones to respond last night though Hilary had no recollection of seeing them there.

"I'm sorry I don't remember you."

"Don't mention it," said Officer Simpkins, the older of the pair. "There was a lot going on last night, and you were injured."

Hilary shifted, trying to sit up straighter in the bed. The movement made her wince, and suddenly Oliver was there at her side, his arm around her shoulders as he adjusted the pillows behind her.

He was so close, his neck mere inches from her face. She inhaled, drawing the scent of him into her nose. Her muscles relaxed and the pain faded as she focused on his nearness and the warmth radiating from his body.

He leaned away and caught her gaze. "Better?"

"Yes," Hilary said, hoping against hope no one had seen her reaction to his proximity. After their discussion about remaining friends, the last thing she wanted was to show how much Oliver affected her body.

"Do you think you can answer a few questions about what happened last night?" asked Officer Simpkins.

"I'll tell you everything I know."

"Should I go?" Oliver asked. The policemen looked at him, but he never glanced away from Hilary. It was clear that regardless of what the police said, he wasn't asking their permission.

He was asking hers.

She appreciated the gesture, his subtle acknowledgment of her privacy. "You can stay," she said, offering him a small smile. "I know you're curious, and you might as well hear about it firsthand."

Oliver nodded and took a few steps away to lean against the far wall. She felt his eyes on her, but now that he'd put a little bit of distance between them, she felt like she could better focus on the police and their questions.

Officer Simpkins removed a small notebook from his pocket, while his partner produced a small recording device. At her nod of consent, Simpkins asked his first question.

"Miss Weston, what happened at the restaurant last night?"

Chapter 5

Oliver leaned against the wall, arms and legs crossed as he listened to Hilary answer questions. She talked about how she and her brother were the only ones left to close up the restaurant, a practice that was apparently common. A growing sense of irritation filled him when he thought about the risks her family asked her to take. He knew from previous conversations with Hilary that she liked her brother, but there were times when he flaked out and left early to go take care of something else. She shouldn't be the only one closing up.

Especially not in her condition.

His eyes flicked to her abdomen once more. Did her family know about the baby? Or was she waiting to tell them once she started to show?

Officer Simpkins asked a question, but Oliver missed it because he wasn't paying attention. He tuned back in as Hilary started to speak.

"Everything was normal," she said. "Jeff was shutting things down in the kitchen, and my parents had gone to make the nightly deposit at the bank. I had just gone to lock the door, when two men barged through. They had guns, and they were wearing masks."

Oliver shifted, the fear in her voice making him wish he could have done something to stop this from happening. If only he'd gotten there earlier! His presence might have deterred the intruders from even trying to break in.

"I screamed," Hilary continued. "I turned and tried to run, but one of them grabbed my arm." She rubbed at a spot on her biceps, the fabric of her hospital gown inching up with the movement. Oliver saw a hint of a bruise on her skin and his blood began to boil. They had *touched* her?

A small part of him was surprised at the intensity of his feelings as he listened to her story. He cared about her as a friend, naturally, but he generally didn't respond like this when hearing about something bad happening to his other friends. When his buddy Carson had been mugged a few months ago, Oliver had been upset but he hadn't been filled with the urge to turn vigilante. Why was Hilary so different?

The urge for justice was a strong Colton streak, as

evidenced by his siblings' responses to his father's crimes. Still, it was a bit surprising to find his feelings were so strong in this situation. He didn't have much time to consider that as she revealed more information. "The man who grabbed me pulled me back against his chest and told me to shut up. The other man yelled for Jeff to come out. I screamed again and told him to run. The man holding me swore and I felt him move behind me. Then it seemed like the back of my head exploded and everything when black."

Rage built inside Oliver as he imagined the scene. Hilary wasn't exactly petite, but he had a good six inches on her. He'd been very aware of her size when they'd been together, and he'd relished the contrast in their relative strength and sizes. The thought that a man had used force to subdue her disgusted him beyond measure.

And the fact that she was pregnant? Made it even worse.

"Did you recognize anything about these guys? The sound of their voices? The way they moved or smelled?"

Hilary shook her head carefully. "No. I'm pretty sure I've never met them before."

The two officers nodded, as if they'd been expecting her to say that.

She looked so small in that bed, so alone. Unable to stand it any longer, Oliver pulled the chair next to her and sat, then reached for her hand. She glanced at him, surprise flashing across her face. But she squeezed his hand in a silent gesture of appreciation.

Touching her, knowing she was safe now helped to calm his anger. He hadn't been able to stop those men last night. But he could make sure she was okay now and keep her safe going forward.

He hesitated slightly at the thought. Was it really his place to protect Hilary? After all, she had someone new in her life. Surely that guy would want to step up, once he knew what had happened. That was probably for the best anyway—he hadn't planned on staying in Blue Larkspur very long. Hilary needed someone consistent in her life right now. Hadn't she basically told him as much yesterday?

"Where is my brother?" she asked. "Have you heard from him? Do you know where he is?"

Simpkins and his partner exchanged a glance. "We're not sure," he said. "He wasn't at the restaurant last night, and your parents tried several times to get in touch with him, but he never responded. We've checked his apartment and several other locations your folks said he frequents. As of right now, he's considered missing."

Hilary sucked in a breath, her eyes going wide. "Is he—" She sniffed, tears welling. "Do you think they killed him?" she finished in a whisper.

Oliver could practically feel the fear radiating off her. He knew she and her brother had had their ups and downs, but he sincerely hoped Jeff wasn't dead.

"We can't say for sure, but I can tell you that there was no evidence of a murder at the restaurant," Simpkins said gently. "Your brother might have been able to get away, or it's possible he went with the men."

Hilary frowned. "Wait, didn't the security cameras capture what happened?"

Simpkins shook his head. "No. We saw two men enter the place thanks to the external cameras. But the camera monitoring the back door to the place had shorted out, and the internal monitoring system had already been turned off by the time the men forced their way inside."

"Dad must have done that before they left," Hilary said dully. "We're supposed to leave the cameras on inside the restaurant overnight, but Dad got it in his head that we could save a few cents on electricity if we don't record all night. Mom told him that was ridiculous, but he's too stubborn to listen."

Simpkins frowned. "They make motion sensor cameras that only start recording if they sense movement."

Hilary lifted one eyebrow. "Yeah. We tried to talk him into making the switch. But he didn't want to spend the money to upgrade the system."

Oliver closed his eyes to hide his exasperation and made a mental note to fund the security upgrade himself. If Hilary was going to continue working there, the place needed to be safe.

"Well, hopefully now your father will consider making the change." Simpkins closed his notebook and returned it to his pocket, and his partner switched off the recording device. "We're going to let you rest now. You've been very helpful. If you can think of any other details, or if you remember something else, please get in touch." He retrieved a business card and handed it to Hilary. "We'll be in touch as we have updates."

"Okay, thank you," Hilary said. "I just hope you can find my brother."

Simpkins nodded. "We're working on it."

The two officers left and Hilary let out a sigh. "I wish I knew what happened to Jeff."

"Has he ever disappeared like this before?" Oliver asked.

"No. He's had his troubles, but as far as I know, no one's ever come after him before." She bit her bottom lip, her eyebrows drawn together. "I just can't imagine what he's done now."

"I'm sure the police will find him soon. Blue Larkspur isn't a huge city. Someone will have heard or seen something."

"I hope you're right." She gave his hand a quick squeeze and pulled away. Oliver released her hand, feeling a small pang at the loss of her touch.

Hilary squinted at the clock on the wall. "When is my doctor stopping by? I'm ready to go home." She reached for the call remote, but Oliver covered it before she could press the button.

"Um, why don't you give them some more time?"

She frowned at him. "Why? I don't think I need to stay here any longer. I'm much better than last night, and I doubt there's anything more they need to do for me."

"You can't be sure about that." She couldn't leave, not until someone had checked out the baby. Why wasn't she more concerned?

"Oliver, what is going on?" She sounded suspicious, which puzzled him. Unless she didn't want to talk about her pregnancy in front of him?

"You know," he hedged. "I just think you should get a thorough work-up before you're released. To make sure *everything* is okay."

He could tell by the look on her face that she didn't know what he was talking about. Either she was truly clueless, or she had a hell of a good poker face.

"Hilary," he tried again. "I know. It's okay—you don't have to pretend with me. I'm not judging you in any way. It's only natural you'd be worried and want to ensure everything is fine before you go home."

She met his gaze, her eyes bright with annoyance. "What are you talking about? What is it that you think you know?"

He gaped at her, wondering why she didn't just acknowledge the truth. "It's… I mean…" For some reason, he was at a loss for words. Finally, he gestured to her stomach. "The baby," he said. "Don't you want to make sure the baby is okay before you leave?"

Hilary leaned back, frowning at him. "That's not

funny." She sounded angry now. "There is no baby. I don't know what you're talking about. I'm going home." She reached for the call button again, but Oliver reflexively pulled it away.

"Hey," she protested, an edge in her voice.

She doesn't know. The realization hit him like a jolt of electricity. Was that even possible? Surely there were signs, changes in her body that made it clear what was happening.

But as he saw the genuine confusion in Hilary's gaze, he knew she truly had no idea.

A weight settled on his shoulders as he realized he needed to tell her. For a split second, Oliver debated on calling in the nurse and letting them break the news. But no. Hilary was his friend, and he didn't want to keep her in the dark any longer than necessary.

Oliver set the call button on the mattress and reached for her hand. "There's something you should know," he said softly, trying to feel his way into this conversation. What was the best way to tell her? How could he break the news without scaring her, or upsetting her further?

"What's going on?" She sounded wary, as though she was bracing for bad news.

Oliver took a deep breath. He usually prided himself on clear communication in his professional life. Why should this be any different?

"Hilary, you're pregnant."

* * *

Hilary stared at Oliver, unable to comprehend his words.

Was this a dream? Was the injury to her head more severe than the doctors initially thought? Surely she wasn't really...?

Her mind shied away from the word, even as her thoughts began to race. "Pregnant?" she whispered.

No. Absolutely not.

Except...

She'd been exhausted lately. Tired on a level that no amount of sleep was able to fix. And she *had* put on a few pounds, despite feeling mildly queasy most days. She'd chalked it all up to the stress of trying to balance school and work, but what if that wasn't the case? What if Oliver was right?

She shook her head slightly, trying to clear her mind. "What makes you say that?" Where had he gotten the idea that she was expecting a baby? He made it sound like her condition was a fact, but she'd never taken a pregnancy test. Maybe he'd seen her curves and come to the wrong conclusion?

That had to be it.

"One of the nurses came in to check on you last night," he said. "She asked me for the name of your obstetrician. Said they needed it for your records, and so they could reach out to her and let her know about the accident. She told me the preliminary exams showed the baby was fine, but you'd still want to follow up with your OB after being released."

"I don't understand," Hilary said.

Confusion flitted across Oliver's face. "What do you mean?"

"How do they know?" *How could they be sure?* Part of her still insisted this was all a mistake, a misunderstanding, even as things started clicking into place.

Oliver shrugged. "They took blood samples from you last night. I guess they ran a pregnancy test as part of their evaluations."

Oh God. Then it must be true.

A strange sense of calm washed over her, making her body numb. Hilary looked down at her belly and realized with a start that her hand was resting on the subtle curve of her abdomen.

"So he doesn't know?" Oliver's deep voice cut through the haze of her shock. He was watching her, a strange expression on his face.

"What?"

"The baby's father." He nodded at her hand. "Are you going to tell him?"

It was a logical question, one that made sense. There was just one problem: Oliver clearly thought her fake boyfriend was the father of her baby. And why shouldn't he? Hilary had made it sound like she had a new man in her life. It was only natural Oliver had connected the dots from her white lie to her current condition.

Looking at him now, Hilary realized she had a choice to make. She could continue her deception, pretend there really was another man in her life and that she was having his baby.

Or she could tell the truth.

She didn't know how Oliver felt about children. He'd mentioned wanting kids at one point, but when they'd talked about it, he'd made it sound like a family was something he planned for in the future. Given his traveling schedule and the demands of his job, he probably wasn't ready to become a father.

Not to mention, once Hilary gave birth, she was going to want to stay in Blue Larkspur. Oh sure, it was theoretically possible to travel with a child, but just the thought of it made her tired. Her parents and friends were here, and she was going to need their support. Oliver seemed like a good guy, but she didn't think he was ready to give up his jet-setting lifestyle in exchange for sleepless nights and dirty diapers.

Maybe it was for the best if he didn't know? They could go their separate ways with him none the wiser. If she told Oliver he was going to be a father, he'd probably feel obligated to her and the baby. Over time, his sense of duty might turn into resentment. And while she could handle being the target of his unhappiness, she didn't want to risk her future child being made to feel unwanted. She didn't like the idea of keeping her baby away from its father, but perhaps it was the right choice in this situation.

But as she looked at Oliver and watched the emotions play across his face, she knew she couldn't do that. As hard as this was going to be, she didn't want her child's life to start with a lie.

"Hilary." He reached for her hand, his expression sympathetic. "If you tell this guy and he runs, he's an idiot. You don't have to do this alone. There are services and organizations that can help, and I can—"

"That's not an issue," she interrupted. The longer she let him talk, the farther away from the truth he got. She had to put a stop to this, before her resolve weakened.

"Oh?" Oliver pulled his hand away. "So you think he'll be happy about the baby? That's great news." He leaned back in the chair, nodding to himself. "Where is he? Should I call him for you? I'm sure he's probably out of his mind with worry since you didn't come home last night."

"Oliver, stop." She shook her head gingerly, the movement and her building emotions making her head ache again.

Her heart began to pound and her stomach cramped as she took a deep breath. This was it. There was no turning back.

Oliver watched her, a slight frown on his face. She met his eyes and opened her mouth, but her throat was so tight she couldn't speak. So she swallowed and tried again.

"The thing is…" Oh, what she wouldn't give for a glass of water! "There is no other man," she finally managed to say. "There never was. I just told you that so you'd leave me alone."

Oliver tilted his head to the side, his frown deepening. "What do you mean?"

"I lied to you yesterday," she said. "I don't have a boyfriend. I haven't slept with anyone since that night I spent with you."

The color drained from Oliver's face. He shot to his feet and began pacing next to the bed, running his hand through his hair. "Are you sure?"

Hilary fought the urge to laugh at the absurd question. "I think that's something I would definitely remember," she said dryly.

Oliver stopped and turned to stare at her, a wild glint in his blue eyes. "But if that's true, then that means… I'm…" He gestured to her belly, clearly at a loss for words.

Hilary nodded, empathizing with his shock. "Yes. The baby is yours."

Chapter 6

No.

It wasn't possible.

Oliver shook his head reflexively, his mind racing.

Why would Hilary say the baby was his? They had used protection!

He looked down at her, a troubling thought creeping into his head. She was a waitress at her family's restaurant, working on her degree at the same time. She wasn't destitute, but she wasn't well-off either. Had the real father of the baby thrown her over, leaving her desperate? Was she trying to make him believe he was responsible so he would step up and take care of them both?

The idea filled him with equal parts pity and disgust. The idea that Hilary would lie to him about something so important... It didn't seem like her at all. But if that was the case, could he really blame her? She was going to have a baby, another person who would be totally dependent on her for survival. Of course she'd do whatever it took to provide for that child.

He met her gaze, expecting to see the glint of challenge in her eyes. But her expression was calm, almost resigned. And unless his missed his guess, there was a faint air of sadness about her.

Almost as if...she was expecting him to walk away.

"I don't understand," he said slowly. "How is it possible that I'm the father?"

She arched an eyebrow. "Was I that forgettable?"

Oliver felt his cheeks heat as he shook his head. "That's not what I meant. We were careful."

Hilary nodded with a quiet sigh. "I know. But here we are."

His knees gave out and he dropped onto the chair by the bed. A baby. He was going to be a father.

His own father's face flashed in his mind, bringing a wave of mixed emotions. He'd thought his dad had been a great guy, until the truth about his misdeeds had come out.

The betrayal had made Oliver doubt every interaction he'd had with his father. Had it been real? Or just another set of lies?

And now Oliver was going to be a father. Was he up to the task? Or would he fail, like his dad?

Oliver dropped his head into his hands, trying to come to terms with the magnitude of this shock.

"You don't have to stay," Hilary said quietly.

He looked over at her. "What?"

"I get it." She glanced away, suddenly very interested in the thin hospital blanket that covered her legs. "It was a fun night, but it wasn't supposed to be anything more. I know you didn't sign up for this."

"Neither did you," he pointed out. "What are you thinking?"

"You mean, am I going to keep it?"

Oliver nodded, holding his breath as he waited for her reply. It wasn't his place to pressure her in any way, but he was curious to know what her plans were.

"I don't think I could go through pregnancy and delivery and then give the baby up for adoption." She shook her head as she spoke. "And at this point, I'm not comfortable with getting an abortion. So yeah, I'm going to have this baby."

Her answer didn't surprise him. Hilary wasn't the type of person to shy away from responsibility.

And neither was he. Not anymore, now that he'd put his teenage hijinks behind him.

So it seemed he had some stepping up to do.

He could do better than his dad.

He had to.

"Okay." He ran his hand over his face, trying to put his thoughts into some type of order. "First things first. You need to see a doctor, to find out if the baby is okay after last night. Then we need to start getting infant stuff, so you'll have what you need later."

"What I'll need?" she echoed. "Does that mean you don't want to be involved?"

"What? No, I—" Oliver's brain derailed as he considered her question. Of course he intended to provide financially for them both. But was he going to go beyond that? Was he going to help with the late-night feedings, the diaper changes, the day-to-day work of caring for an infant?

To his surprise, the idea wasn't totally unappealing. He understood babies were a lot of work and required constant care. He'd spent a little time with his niece Iris and knew from talking to Rachel and James that parenting was a full-time job. The thought of foisting all of that onto Hilary didn't sit right with him. But how much could he really help, given the demands of his career? It was hard to stay connected when traveling.

A sense of possessiveness grew inside him as he looked at the subtle curve of her abdomen. This was *his* baby, too. Being a father meant more than bringing home a paycheck. What kind of dad would he be if he wasn't there to bond with his kid?

His own dad had made terrible choices to financially support the family. Oliver vowed silently that he wasn't going to follow in his footsteps.

"I do want to help," he said finally. He'd figure out a way to balance his job and help out. Men did it all the time; he could make it work, too. "I'm just not sure how much you're going to want me around." Like she'd said before, they hadn't made promises to each other that night. It was entirely possible Hilary might want nothing to do with him. But if that was the case, Oliver wasn't simply going to walk away. He wanted to know his child, so they would have to work together, no matter what.

Something flashed in Hilary's eyes—surprise? Gratitude? He wasn't sure. But before they could continue the conversation, there was a short rap at the door and a doctor walked in.

"Good morning, I'm Dr. Hutchins." She was short, with chin-length salt-and-pepper hair and a ready smile. "How are you feeling today, Miss Weston?"

"Uh, I'm okay." Hilary shifted on the bed, trying to sit up. Without thinking, Oliver stepped forward to help arrange the pillows behind her back. His hand grazed the nape of her neck and the warmth of her skin sent tingles shooting up his arm.

He sucked in a breath, confused by his body's reaction to a simple brush of skin against skin. What was the matter with him?

"My head is still achy," Hilary continued. "But I feel much better than I did last night."

"That's good," the doctor said. "I'm not sure how much you remember, but when you were brought in last night, you had a pretty nasty gash on the back of your head. They stitched you up in the emergency room and did a CT scan to examine your head, since you had lost consciousness."

Hilary nodded. "The stitches itch a little."

Dr. Hutchins smiled. "That's normal. They will probably itch for a few days as the skin heals. Your CT scan was normal, which is a good sign. No hematomas or broken bones. You experienced a mild concussion, so you're going to want to take it easy for the next several days. Do you live with someone, or have someone who can stay with you?"

"No," Hilary responded, just as Oliver replied, "Yes."

The doctor looked from her to Oliver, then back again. "I see," she said. "Sounds like there's a disagreement here?"

"I live alone," Hilary clarified.

"You can stay with me," Oliver said. Hilary began to frown, so he pressed ahead. "There is plenty of room in my suite. You can take one bedroom and I'll use the other. It'll be fine."

"Can't I just go home?" Hilary looked at the doctor, clearly hoping for support.

Dr. Hutchins shook her head. "I'm afraid you do need someone with you, at least for a few days."

Hilary looked like she wanted to argue. "Fine," she muttered, obviously unhappy. "I'll call my mom."

"Don't be ridiculous," Oliver said. "Your parents are already dealing with your brother and the break-in at the restaurant. It's no trouble to have you stay with me. You don't even have to talk to me—there's enough room that we don't have to see each other at all."

Hilary pressed her lips together in a thin line. "All right." She crossed her arms and looked down.

Dr. Hutchins studied her carefully. "Are you certain? You don't have to go anywhere you don't want to."

Oliver realized the doctor was getting the wrong impression. "Hilary, it's okay. I'm not trying to force you. If you don't want to stay with me, I can hire someone to help you out at your home."

"No," Hilary said, shaking her head. "It's fine." She glanced up at him. "I appreciate the offer. I'll stay with you. We have a lot to discuss."

He nodded, relief washing over him. Until that moment, he hadn't realized how much he wanted to be the one to watch over her.

Dr. Hutchins smiled, apparently satisfied. "That's settled, then. You'll need to take it easy for the next several days. No alcohol, light meals. Try to rest your brain as much as possible. That means limited television or screen time of any kind, and little to no reading."

Hilary winced. "It's going to be hard to cut back on reading, but I'll do it."

"The more you try to push yourself, the longer it will take for you to feel normal again," said the doctor. "I recommend giving your brain a break so it can heal."

"I will," Hilary replied.

"Do you have any questions for me?"

Oliver bit his tongue to keep from speaking over Hilary. He had lots of questions, most of them centered on the baby and if it was all right after Hilary's injury.

Fortunately, she seemed to be thinking the same thing. "I didn't realize I was pregnant," she said, twin spots of color appearing high on her cheeks. "Is the baby okay?"

"As far as we know, yes," said Dr. Hutchins. "I take it you don't have an OB?"

Hilary shook her head. "No. Like I said, this was a huge surprise."

The doctor's laugh was light and genuine. "Trust me, you're not the first patient to have this shock. I'll put the names and numbers of some local obstetricians in your discharge paperwork. I recommend you call for an appointment soon after you get home. I don't think the baby was affected by your accident, but you'll want to start getting prenatal care before you get much farther along in your pregnancy."

Hilary's hand rested lightly on her abdomen, a seemingly unconscious gesture that made Oliver's heart do a funny little flip inside his chest. He still couldn't believe he was going to be a father! Hopefully he and Hilary could talk while she rested in his hotel suite. They had a lot to discuss, and while she was under doctor's orders to take it easy, he didn't want to waste this time they were going to have together.

After a few more instructions, Dr. Hutchins left the room, promising to sign off on the discharge paperwork soon. After the door had closed behind her, Hilary let out a breath and turned to look at him, her expression troubled.

She didn't speak right away, and Oliver wasn't sure what to say. After the shock they'd both experienced this morning, the quiet felt like the aftermath of a storm.

Finally, he broke the silence. "I meant what I said earlier."

Hilary gave him a puzzled look. "About the hotel," he clarified. "I don't want to make you uncomfortable about being around me. There really is a ton of room." The last thing he wanted was for her to feel trapped with him. The doctor hadn't said anything about stress, but surely that wouldn't be good for her head or the baby.

"Honestly? I'm not worried about that right now."

"Oh?" Then why did she seem upset? From what he'd just heard the doctor say, she was going to make a full recovery and the baby was fine. Both of those things sounded like good news to him...

"I don't think I can focus on anything until we know what happened to my brother." Hilary blinked hard and Oliver mentally kicked himself for temporarily forgetting why she'd landed in the hospital in the first place. It was only natural she was worried about Jeff! He was missing, and no one seemed to know where he was.

Oliver wasn't a detective, but he might still be able to help. After all, he had family connections to law enforcement. There might be a few strings he could pull to get answers for Hilary. If it would ease her mind so they could talk about the baby, so much the better.

"Let me help," he suggested. "I can make some calls, find out if any of my connections knows anything."

Her eyes widened as she looked up at him. "You'd do that?"

Oliver nodded. "Of course. We're still friends, right? That's what friends do for each other."

"Right," Hilary echoed. "Friends." She sounded doubtful, and he realized she didn't think he was being totally sincere.

Her suspicion stung, but he brushed it aside. Right now, this wasn't about him. He was going to be a father, and at this moment, the best thing he could do for his child was to step up and support Hilary. They needed to work together to effectively parent their kid, and they were starting from square one. Fortunately, they still had several months before the baby arrived, but they couldn't afford to procrastinate when it came to settling things between them. He wanted to be on a good, solid footing with Hilary when she went into labor.

It would take a while to build trust between them. Fortunately, Oliver made a living from forging connections with people. He could do the same thing with Hilary.

One small step at a time.

You have got to be kidding me.

Hilary stepped into Oliver's penthouse suite at the Metropolitan Hotel and stopped after a few steps, standing in what could only be described as the foyer.

What kind of suite had a foyer? Her own apartment didn't even have one!

She heard the click of Oliver's shoes as he walked behind her on the marble tile and he stopped next to her, her bag in hand. They'd gone to her place after she'd been discharged from the hospital, where she'd packed a duffel with toiletries and clothes. Normally, she was proud of her small yet cozy apartment, but seeing the opulence of this place made her feel a little embarrassed in comparison. Oliver must think she lived in a slum, if these were his normal accommodations.

"Everything okay?" he asked.

She nodded, her gaze landing on the small round table in the center of the space, a large vase filled with fresh flowers sitting atop. A few feet beyond, the marble tile transitioned to cream colored carpet, and there was a step down into the interior of the suite.

"This place is really fancy," she said, thinking back to their night together. He'd had a room at the

Metropolitan then, too, but it hadn't been nearly as luxurious.

He glanced around. "Yeah, my normal room was booked, so they upgraded me to the penthouse." His broad shoulders shrugged, as though this type of thing happened all the time. Maybe for him, it did. "It's too big for just me, but I'm glad to have the space now that you'll be staying here for a few days."

Oliver walked past her and stepped into the living room. "Let me show you the bedroom. There's a decent-sized closet, so you can hang up your clothes."

Hilary followed him, her feet sinking into the thick nap of the carpet as he led her through the living room and down a short hall. He stepped into an enormous bedroom and she once again had to remind herself not to gape at the lavishness on display.

Oliver set her bag on an ottoman at the foot of the king-size four-poster bed. Then he turned to face her.

"The closet is over there," he said, gesturing to a closed door on the left wall. "And over here is the bathroom." He walked to a set of French doors and pulled them open, revealing a sea of gray marble tile and an oversize claw-foot bathtub. The far wall was lined with frosted-glass windows, making the room effortlessly bright. A walk-in shower sat in the corner, and in the other corner an outcropping of the wall created a small enclave of privacy for the toilet.

Oliver walked over to the countertop and gathered his toiletries. "I'll put these in the other bathroom, so you can have this one to yourself."

The *other* bathroom? There was a second one?

"I'll move my clothes, too," he continued. "I want you to feel like this is your home while you're here. Please use the space just like you would your own bedroom."

It was a nice thought, but Hilary wasn't sure she could relax in the face of all this wealth. The vase in the entryway alone probably cost more than her monthly rent! If she accidentally damaged or broke something, it would wipe out her savings to replace it. And now that she was going to have a baby, she couldn't afford to waste money like that.

"Do you think this will be okay?"

She glanced at Oliver, surprised by the look of shy uncertainty on his face. He was always so cool and composed, but in this moment, he seemed genuinely worried that she might not think the room was good enough.

A wave of tenderness hit her, along with the urge to cup the side of his face with her hand. His apparent concern made her feel special. For a brief instant, she wanted to hold him and assure him that it was fine. If she let herself, she could pretend he was truly interested in looking after her, and not just worried about the baby.

But she wasn't going to make that mistake. Oliver had made it clear he was only interested in her as a friend, nothing more. Everything he did now was to make sure their baby was okay. And while she appreciated the fact that he was trying to step up and do the right thing, the fact that he probably saw her as a glorified incubator stung a little.

She pasted on a smile. "This is amazing," she said. "More than I could ask for." In fact, the suite was definitely bigger than her own apartment, a fact he had to recognize since he'd seen her place.

He looked relieved. "If there's anything you need, let me know. The hotel staff is outstanding, and if there's something they can't do, I certainly can."

Hilary nodded, having no intention of asking the staff for anything. She'd always done things for herself, and she wasn't about to stop now. But she wasn't going to point that out. Oliver would probably tell her that she needed to rest, and she didn't feel like arguing right now. "Thank you," she said.

Oliver glanced at his watch. "We still have a couple of hours before it'll be time for dinner. Would you like to unpack and get settled here while I make a few calls?"

A spark of hope flared to life in Hilary's chest at Oliver's words. She knew it was a long shot, but maybe one of his connections would have news about the investigation into Jeff's disappearance? She'd talked to her mom briefly on the way to the hotel, and she knew her parents were out of their minds with worry. They'd closed the restaurant for the next few days, unable to work while Jeff was missing. Hilary kept expecting her phone to ring and to hear Jeff on the other end of the line saying, "Surprise!" What she wouldn't give for this to be a horrible joke!

"That sounds great," she said, resisting the urge to push him out of the room so he could get started. Part of her wanted to stay with him while he spoke with his connections, but she was so tired. Plus, her presence might make him feel like he had to censor his questions so as not to worry her. Right now, she needed information, no matter what it might reveal.

"Okay. I'll remove my clothes from the closet a bit later. There's enough space that you should still have plenty of room for your own stuff." He stopped at the threshold of the door to the bedroom. "Please try to relax. I'll tell you what I find out, and we can think about next steps then. And dinner," he added with a small smile. "You didn't eat much in the hospital. You must be hungry."

Truth be told, she wasn't. But Hilary knew she needed to eat, for the baby if not herself. "I will be," she said.

He searched her face and she saw the worry in his eyes. "Let me know if you need anything," he said. "I'm just in the other room."

"I'm fine. Really," she assured him. "And I'll be much better once we know more about Jeff."

"I can't promise anything," Oliver began, but she raised her hand to cut him off.

"I know. I'm just grateful you're trying." Even if he didn't learn anything new, at least she could comfort herself with the knowledge she'd done everything possible to find out where her brother was.

Oliver left the room, closing the door quietly behind him. Now that she was alone, Hilary felt her body relax. Being around Oliver wasn't stressful, per se, but it seemed like her body was always aware of him, her muscles slightly tense in anticipation of any move he might make.

She walked to the ottoman and toed off her shoes, then pulled her phone from her purse. There was a sitting area with two large chairs and a table to the left of the bed, and she sank into the padded embrace of the recliner with a sigh. Her aches and pains from the fall and a night spent on the hard hospital mattress began to ease and she realized just how tired she was.

But she couldn't sleep just yet. She had responsibilities to take care of first.

She pulled up her email and messaged her professors, telling them she'd had a medical and family emergency. Hopefully they would extend her deadlines accordingly, but at this point, she didn't care either way. Her priorities right now were to find her brother and figure out how she was going to handle having this baby in a few months.

Staring at the small screen and trying to focus on typing made her head twinge painfully. She set her phone on the table and rubbed her forehead, hoping this wasn't the beginning of a bad headache.

The large bed looked so inviting, but Hilary couldn't bring herself to lie on those clean white sheets until she'd washed away the residue of the hospital. So she forced herself to get up and headed to the bathroom.

Unable to resist the temptation of that big tub, she started to run a bath. A set of fancy toiletries sat on a shelf nearby and she took a sniff from one of the bottles. A light, citrus scent hit her nose, appealing and fresh. She added a dollop of the soap to the running water, triggering a froth of bubbles.

She undressed while the tub filled. The back of her head was tender, and she gently probed the area around her stitches. Shampoo was out of the question, or so the doctor had told her. But she could rinse her hair now and start using soap after two days.

Hilary slipped into the tub and stuck her head under the running water. Her injury stung as the water hit it, but she sucked in a breath and massaged the dried blood out of her hair. The pain was a small price to pay to feel clean again.

That done, she switched off the water and leaned back, submerging herself in the warm bubbles. She closed her eyes, her hand drifting to her belly and resting there.

Pregnant.

She still couldn't quite believe it.

She'd thought about kids before, figuring they would be part of her future. *Future* being the important word. But it seemed she was going to have to adjust her timetable in that respect.

For the past few months, she'd thought the changes in her body were due to stress. Learning about the baby felt a little bit like a betrayal, as though her body had been up to something behind her back. Hilary had always assumed that she was in control of her life. For the first time, she was forced to acknowledge that wasn't really the case.

Then there was the matter of Oliver. Never in a million years had she imagined their night together would result in a baby. Neither of them had been looking for anything serious. Sure, maybe she had indulged in a short-lived fantasy of having a future with Oliver, but not like this.

How were they going to work this out? Her life was here, in Blue Larkspur, while he lived out of hotels most of the time. She didn't know much about his family, beyond what his local siblings were doing with the Truth Foundation. Were they close? Estranged? What had his childhood been like? What kind of relationship had he had with his father? He'd told her a bit about his wilder years, and he'd definitely straightened up and made something of himself. Would he be a strict dad? Or permissive? Were they going to be a real team, or was he going to be the fun parent while she was stuck being the disciplinarian?

If only she had a crystal ball!

The attack, the baby, her missing brother… Under normal circumstances, it would border on overwhelming. But now that she was dealing with a head injury, she simply couldn't handle it.

She shifted and took a deep breath, determined

to clear her mind. One thing at a time. That was the only way she'd get through this.

Moving her limbs under the water, she decided to try a stress-relief technique a friend had told her about. She focused on her toes, relaxing each muscle before moving to her ankles.

By the time she got to her hips, a pleasant floating sensation had taken over, leaving her feeling almost light-headed. Her thoughts seemed to move in slow motion, drifting like jellyfish in the sea of her consciousness.

With a sigh, Hilary released her grip on her worries and bobbed along with them.

Chapter 7

Oliver sank onto the plush sofa with a sigh and ran a hand through his hair, trying to organize his thoughts. He'd spent the last few hours worried about Hilary and adjusting to the news of her pregnancy, but now he had to switch gears and think about her brother and his predicament.

Knowing she was in the next room helped ease his mind. Finding her on the floor of the restaurant last night had left him shaken, and he was still concerned about her recovery. Despite her apparent doubts about his intentions, he would have offered to have her stay with him even if she wasn't carrying his baby.

There was another benefit to keeping her close: it

would be easier for them to talk about where to go from here. They had a lot of decisions to make and being in close proximity would hopefully help them reach a place where they could talk freely about what they each wanted. If he was being honest, Oliver was a little intimidated by the thought of having these discussions with Hilary. His past relationships had been enjoyable and on the lighter side, two people coming together for some fun while it suited them both. But thanks to the baby, he and Hilary were now going to be joined forever. She was going to be a permanent fixture in his life, and he couldn't keep her at arm's length forever. Not if they were truly going to work together.

The idea of opening himself up to her was enough to make his stomach twist. But he couldn't think about that now—he'd promised to make some calls on her behalf, and he needed to follow through. Hopefully, this would be the first step in building trust between them.

He pulled out his phone and scrolled through his contacts until he landed on the name Philip Rees. Philip was a police detective in nearby Boulder who had recently started dating Oliver's younger sister, Naomi. Oliver didn't expect Jeff's disappearance would be a major concern for the Boulder Police Department, but Philip had a few friends in BLPD who might be willing to provide some insider details on the investigation.

Philip answered on the second ring. "Rees."

"Hey, it's Oliver Colton."

"What's up, man?" A friendly note entered Philip's voice. "You doing okay?"

"Yeah, I'm fine. But a situation has come up here, and I'm wondering if you might have a minute to spare?"

"Ah, sure. What's going on?"

Oliver launched into a recap of Hilary's assault last night, and the fact that her brother was now missing. "I don't know a lot about the guy, but according to his sister and his parents, it's unusual for him to disappear."

"Are the police treating this like a kidnapping?" Philip asked.

"I'm not sure," Oliver admitted. "A guy by the name of Simpkins interviewed me last night and came to the hospital for Hilary's statement this morning. But he didn't say what the police are thinking, or how they're planning to investigate."

"This hasn't come up on my radar," Philip said. "But it might later, depending on how BLPD decides to handle things. I can make a few calls, ask around and see if anyone knows anything."

"That would be great," Oliver said. "I appreciate anything you can share."

"No problem," Philip replied. "Sit tight. I'll get back to you as soon as I know something."

Oliver ended the call and thumbed over to his brother's number. He hesitated before tapping the screen. There was so much he wanted to share with

Dominic, but should he tell him about the baby yet? Dom was busy building a life for himself and Sami and adjusting to his new work for the FBI. And while Oliver had no qualms about asking his brother for a favor, he didn't want to use Dom as an unofficial therapist, especially when he was still figuring out how he felt about things.

No, he decided. He'd ask Dom to help out with Jeff, but he wouldn't tell his family about Hilary's pregnancy until they had had a chance to really talk to each other first.

"'Sup, broseph?"

Oliver rolled his eyes at the greeting. "Hey. I need a favor."

"Go."

Oliver's heart warmed at his brother's response. That was Dom—dependable, no-nonsense, always there. Oliver was on good terms with all of his siblings, but he was closest to Dom and Ezra. As triplets, the three of them shared a tight bond. He could call either one of them and know that his brothers would drop everything if he needed help, just as he'd do the same for them.

He described the situation again. To his credit, Dom listened without interrupting him. When he finished, his brother took a deep breath.

"Well. You always did have a nose for trouble."

"Hey," Oliver protested. "I may have had my issues in the past, but I'm on the side of the angels now."

"Sure," Dom replied, his tone heavy with sarcasm. "What do you need me to do?"

"I was hoping you could do a little digging on your end and see if you can learn any info about the investigation. The officer in charge seems kind of old-school, and I don't think he's going to share details unless he learns something big."

"I'll see what I can do," Dom said. "I haven't seen any bulletins about a kidnapping, so they might be treating it as a missing person case. But I'll ask around."

"Appreciate it," Oliver replied. A sense of relief washed over him now that his brother had agreed to help. As an FBI agent, Dom was a skilled investigator who knew his way around a case. If there was any information to be found, Dom would uncover it.

"How's life behind a desk?" Oliver teased. After his cover had been blown a few months ago, Dom had retired from undercover work. Their mother was thrilled at the change as it drastically lessened the risks he was forced to take as part of his job.

"It's an adjustment," Dom said. "But having Sami's support makes it a lot easier." Warmth entered Dom's voice at the mention of Sami, his fiancée. Oliver was happy for his brother, glad he'd found someone to share his life with. He pushed aside a twinge of wistfulness; both of his brothers had recently found love. In Ezra's case, he'd stepped into a paternal role with Theresa's kids as well. Oliver made a mental note to talk to his brother soon. Ezra would likely have some tips for him, and his brother usually gave good advice.

"Let me know when you guys set a date," Oliver said.

"I will," Dom said. "And don't think you're going to get off that easy."

"What do you mean?" Oliver asked.

"I have questions for you. Like what were you doing, going back to Atria after it closed? And why are you so invested in this Jeff character? This isn't the type of thing you'd normally worry about."

Oliver shifted, uncomfortable at being the focus of Dom's attention. "I'm just trying to help out a friend."

"A friend, huh? You sure there's not more to it? I seem to remember you mentioning a certain waitress the last time we were all in town."

It was on the tip of Oliver's tongue to tell Dom everything—about his night with Hilary and the shocking news of her pregnancy. But he couldn't bring himself to do it just yet. Talking about the baby with anyone other than Hilary felt like a bit of a betrayal at this point. He didn't want to jeopardize things with her by making her think he'd been spilling the news before she had a chance to decide how she wanted to share it. It was his baby, too, but since she was the one expecting, she'd get all the attention, both the good and the bad.

"You know I'm always on the go," Oliver said lightly. "What woman is going to want to be with me, when I'm never in one place for long?" He tried to play it off as a joke, but the truth was his near constant travel schedule was starting to grow old. He'd been toying with the idea of slowing down and establishing a home base for the last several months. Now that he was going to be a father, the thought seemed even more appealing.

Dom laughed. "I'm sure there are lots of ladies who would love to live the life of a jet-setter. You just haven't found the right one yet."

"Guess I'll have to keep looking." The image of Hilary's face immediately came to mind, as though his subconscious was casting a vote. The trouble was, she hadn't exactly been thrilled to see him. The discovery that she was carrying his child didn't seem to have helped matters.

"Well, while you work on your love life I'll start asking around and see if I can come up with any information about Jeff."

"Thank you," Oliver said. "You always were my favorite brother."

Dom laughed, "I'm glad to hear it. But don't hold your breath. I have to be careful about who I talk to. Local police generally don't appreciate getting calls from the FBI regarding their active cases, especially if they haven't requested assistance."

"I don't expect you to start any drama. I was hoping you had some friends who would talk to you unofficially."

"I have a few names in mind," Dom said. "I just want you to manage your expectations here."

"Consider them managed," Oliver assured his brother.

After a little more back-and-forth, he ended the call. Was there anything else he could do to help find Jeff?

For a second, he considered calling the police chief himself due to the growing connection between Chief Lawson and Oliver's mother, Isa. And though Oliver himself had known the older man for years, he quickly dismissed the idea of contacting the chief directly. Officer Simpkins would definitely not appreciate Oliver going over his head like that, and Lawson might take offense as well. No, better to let things play out for a bit. If there were no signs of progress soon, he could always make the call.

He placed his phone on the nearby table and leaned back on the sofa once more. But his thoughts were too unsettled to remain still for long. Standing, Oliver walked over to the nearby bank of windows and looked out over the mountains dappled by the late afternoon sun.

Jeff was out there somewhere. Hopefully they'd find him alive and unharmed, but given the events of last night, Oliver had his doubts about the latter. Whatever the outcome, he needed answers soon. Hilary had already been through so much, and the stress of worrying about her brother couldn't be good for the baby.

His stomach rumbled quietly, a reminder that while his mind was preoccupied, his body still had needs. Oliver glanced at his watch—it was a little after five. The calls had taken longer than he'd thought.

Hilary must be hungry, too, he thought, heading for her bedroom. He knocked softly at the door and waited for her response, but the room within remained quiet. Another knock, this time a little louder.

Still no response. *Maybe she's asleep?* He hated to wake her, but he didn't want her to miss a meal, especially since she'd only nibbled on a bit of food while in the hospital. Moving quietly, he opened her door. No sense barging in and scaring her out of a nap.

He entered cautiously. The curtains were still mostly drawn across the window on the far wall, making the room somewhat dim.

His eyes cut to the bed, expecting to see Hilary curled up asleep. But she wasn't there. Puzzled, he crossed the room and stopped just outside the bathroom.

"Hilary?"

Silence.

Worry built in his chest. He knew she hadn't left the suite—she would have had to walk past him to do that, and he would have seen her. No, she was still here and since she wasn't in the bed, she had to be in the bathroom.

He knew she would kill him if he invaded her

privacy. But why hadn't she responded to her name? What if she had fallen again and wasn't able to reply?

Oliver's heart began to pound hard in his chest as he imagined Hilary lying motionless on the bathroom tiles. It wasn't hard for him to picture it, since he'd found her like that just last night.

He said her name one last time, still reluctant to invade her space. He'd promised her she wouldn't have to be near him, but this was starting to feel like an emergency.

"Hilary, I'm coming inside."

He gave her a few seconds, then entered the bathroom.

There she was. Reclining in the large bathtub, her body stretched out and her eyes closed.

Oliver froze, feeling a bit like a deer caught in the headlights of an oncoming car. He couldn't see anything beyond the profile of her face and the slope of her neck, but there was something so peaceful about her expression that he couldn't look away.

After a moment, he released the breath he didn't realize he'd been holding. Hilary made no move in his direction, showed no acknowledgment of his presence.

She's asleep, he realized with a start.

Unable to help himself, Oliver took one step closer, than another. He needed to wake her, and it was clear from his previous attempts that simply calling her name from a distance wasn't going to cut it.

Was she not responding because she was exhausted from last night? Or was this a consequence of her head injury?

Keeping his eyes glued to her face, he knelt by the side of the tub. A few stray bubbles dotted the surface, remnants of what had likely been a large froth earlier in her bath.

The water had a hazy quality, thanks to the lingering soap and the light filtering through the frosted-glass windows. Oliver glanced around for a nearby towel and caught sight of her body.

His breath hitched as he took in the view. She was beautiful, all stretched out and totally relaxed. His palms tingled as he remembered running his hands over her, cupping her breasts and hips.

Even though he'd only been with her once, he could see the subtle changes of her body. Her curves were more pronounced, and she looked…softer, somehow. He looked at her lower abdomen and his stomach did a little flip as he noticed the beginnings of a telltale bump.

We did that, he marveled. A sense of wonder came over him as he stared at the gentle swell, wanting so badly to touch her, to touch their baby.

After a moment, he shook his head and refocused. He'd come in here to wake Hilary, not stare at her nude body like some kind of creeper. And even though seduction was not on his mind—well, not at the top of his mind—she wouldn't appreciate knowing he'd violated her privacy.

He turned so that he was facing her. Then he knelt down, reached out and placed a hand on her shoulder.

"Hilary," he said softly. "Wake up."

He jostled her gently, hoping the movement would help rouse her.

It did. She stirred at his voice, frowning slightly as she slowly opened her eyes.

"Oliver? What—?"

He could tell the instant she realized where she was. Her eyes went wide, and she jerked upright to fold her body, sending a little water splashing over the side of the tub. It hit him in the chest and soaked his lap.

"Oh my God," she exclaimed. "What are you doing in here?"

Oliver held up his hands. "I came to check on you. You didn't respond when I knocked or when I called out. I was worried something had happened and you were hurt."

"Well, I'm not," she said, an edge to her tone. "I just fell asleep, that's all."

"I noticed. Normally, I wouldn't bother you. But I'm hungry and I thought you might be, too. You didn't eat much in the hospital today, and I didn't want you to go all night without food."

Hilary frowned at him, her arms wrapped around her knees. "What time is it?"

He shrugged. "Probably five thirty or close to six at this point."

She gaped. "What? Surely I haven't been asleep

that long!" She shivered slightly, a testament to her now-cool bathwater.

"Afraid so," he replied.

She looked at him for a long moment, then released her grip on her legs and unfolded her body. Before he knew what she was doing, she gripped the edges of the tub and stood up, towering over him.

Oliver tilted his head back, his mouth going dry at the sight. He didn't try to close his eyes or glance away—through her actions, Hilary had given him tacit permission to look his fill. His gaze ran over her hungrily, taking in everything. Beads of water raced over her skin, leaving traces of rivulets across the slope of her breasts and dripping off the tips of her nipples, which had stiffened in response to the cold air of the bathroom.

Oliver swallowed hard, heat suffusing him as he imagined following the path of those droplets with his tongue.

Was she trying to torture him?

He looked at her face and saw a glint of defiance in her eyes. Almost as if she was daring him to say something.

"Let me get you a towel," he croaked.

He managed to get to his feet and stiffly moved to the stack that was arranged on one of the counters. If she wanted to give him a hard time, he could give it right back to her. He grabbed one and turned around, offering a slow, deliberate smile as he handed her the towel. "I wasn't expecting a show tonight, but I'll take it."

Hilary blinked and blushed as she unfolded the towel. "You've seen it all before," she muttered.

He took her hand to steady her as she stepped over the edge of the tub. "Not like this," he said gently, dropping the flirtation.

She glanced up at him, a hint of vulnerability in her eyes.

"Do you feel different?" he asked, still holding her hand. "I mean, now that you know you're pregnant?"

"A little," she admitted softly. Her free hand drifted to her abdomen, resting on the towel that she'd wrapped around her body.

Oliver's eyes tracked the motion. "Has it moved yet?"

"I don't know," she replied. "I mean, probably? But I haven't been able to feel anything yet."

He nodded, still focused on her hand. He wanted so badly to touch her, but he didn't dare ask.

Apparently, he didn't need to. Hilary reached for his wrist and drew him toward her. Before Oliver realized what was happening, she pressed his palm to the gentle swell, resting her hand over his.

A shock zinged up his arm. Even though he wasn't touching her directly, he felt profoundly connected to her.

And their baby.

The curve was firm and solid under his fingers, which was surprising. Up until that moment, he'd thought her bump would be soft, not hard. It was a visceral reminder that she was sharing her body with someone else, an entirely new person they had created together.

Oliver blinked as tears stung his eyes. Even though he couldn't feel the fetus moving inside her, he'd never felt so attuned to another human being. It was the most intimate experience of his life, and he couldn't find the words to express all of the emotions this simple touch had stirred up inside of him.

A sense of resolve filled him, pushing out any lingering doubts and fears. He was going to be here for this child. He would be a real and present father, not some absentee dad who dropped in when his schedule permitted. A small twinge of fear reverberated through his mind as he thought of his own father. The pressures of providing for his family had led his dad to do terrible things. Right now, Oliver couldn't imagine following in his footsteps, but he already knew he'd do anything for this baby. Still, that didn't mean he was destined to make the same kind of mistakes...

He shook off the disturbing feeling and glanced up, wondering if Hilary was equally affected by this moment. She was watching him with a look of tenderness on her face that warmed his heart. They still had a lot of issues to work out between them, but he felt closer to her now, more confident that they could find a path forward. It wasn't going to be easy, but as long as they kept their little family in mind, he knew they could forge a compromise.

Oliver swallowed, pushing down the lump in his throat. "Thank you," he said hoarsely.

Hilary smiled. "One day she'll move for us."

"She?" He latched on to the word, his brain also registering that she'd used the word *us*. "Do you already know it's a girl?" The doctor hadn't said anything about the baby's sex, but maybe someone had mentioned it to Hilary when he'd been getting coffee or had stepped out of the room.

Hilary shook her head. "No, it's just a feeling."

Oliver decided to tease her a little. "And here I was feeling like it was a boy."

She chuckled, then froze. "Would you be disappointed? If it turns out you have a daughter, not a son?"

Oliver didn't stop to think. He pulled Hilary to his chest and wrapped his arms around her. "Oh God, not at all. I don't care either way. I just want them to be okay. And you, too," he added softly, giving her a little squeeze.

He felt her relax against him, her arms coming up to link around his waist. "That's good," she sighed. They stood there for a moment, not speaking, enjoying the silence. For the first time in a long time, Oliver felt a sense of peace.

A fine tremor ran through Hilary's body, and he realized she was cold. "Come on," he said, releasing her and taking her hand. "You're freezing. You need to get dressed." He led her into the bedroom, then released her and walked to the door. "Join me when you're ready. We'll decide what do to about dinner."

Hilary nodded, and he turned and headed into the living room area before he did something wild, like step back over there and kiss her.

It was going to be hard, keeping his feelings for Hilary to himself. Even now, he could feel his growing attachment to the baby increasing his attraction to her. Not simply because she was carrying his child though that didn't hurt. No, just being around her reignited the spark he'd experienced the first time he'd seen her.

But that was his problem. And he'd figure out a way to deal with it.

They decided on pizza and salad. Oliver called the order in, and while they waited, Hilary called her parents. She hadn't spoken to them since last night, and her memories of seeing them were a little fuzzy. Oliver had spoken to them just before she'd been released from the hospital, but she wanted to check in with them herself.

"Honey, how are you feeling?" her father asked.

She shifted in the chair, drawing her legs up and to the side. "I'm okay, Dad. Still a little sore, but otherwise fine."

"I'll never forgive myself for having those cameras switched off." She heard the note of anguish in his voice and knew he must feel guilty about his insistence on saving a few dollars at the expense of security. If the cameras inside the restaurant had been filming, the police might have already been able to find the men who assaulted her and took Jeff.

"Any updates from the police?" she asked. It was a long shot—they'd only been working to locate Jeff for a day. But maybe someone had seen something?

"No," he said, confirming her fears. His sigh was heavy. "Your mother isn't handling this well. Between your injuries and Jeff's disappearance, she's been in bed most of the day."

"You can tell her I'm okay," Hilary said. "Hopefully that will help make her feel better." Given everything going on at the moment, now wasn't the time to announce her pregnancy. She wanted it to be happy news, not something that added to her mother's stress. Besides, better to tell them in person. A development like this was worth a face-to-face conversation.

Would she have been able to do that with Oliver? The thought appeared from nowhere, forcing her to wonder about what would have happened if she hadn't been attacked last night. She would have eventually realized she was pregnant, of course. But at that point, Oliver likely would have been gone from Blue Larkspur, off on another business trip. She'd have been forced to tell him over the phone, if he'd ever bothered to return her calls. Given his recent track record of silence after their hookup, she had to question if they would have ever seen each other again. She'd given him the brush-off at dinner last night and would have done it again if she hadn't been unconscious when he'd turned up at the restaurant. It was easy to imagine Oliver walking away for good after that.

She glanced at him now, wondering at the turn of events that had led them to this moment. In some ways, maybe the attack had been a good thing? Finding out about the baby had been a shock, but at least Oliver knew about it, too. She didn't have to try to track him down or tell him he was going to be a father via email or text message. Would he have even believed her, if he hadn't spoken to her in person, seen the truth on her face?

Fortunately, she didn't have to wonder. But she couldn't deny that part of her worried about how things would have been different, had she not learned about the baby until the pregnancy was farther along.

The sound of her father's voice interrupted her musings. "—wish I knew what had happened to your brother."

Guilt speared her as she realized she'd been more worried about her own situation—which while life-changing, was stable for the moment—than her missing brother. Someone had taken Jeff, and given what they'd done to her, it was a safe bet they weren't treating him gently.

"Do you have any idea why someone wanted to grab him?" Jeff had seemed troubled over the last few weeks, but he'd never talked to Hilary about his problems. Maybe he had shared his worries with their dad?

Her father hesitated a second before answering. "No, I can't imagine who would have done this."

Hilary frowned; he hadn't really answered her question. But before she could press him on it, there was a knock at the door of the suite.

Oliver stepped out of the room and she heard him speak as he answered the door. A few seconds later, a hotel attendant wheeled a serving trolley over to the large dining table in the space adjacent to the sitting area.

Hilary watched as the young man set the table with plates, napkins and silverware. Then he added a large salad bowl and a platter covered by a silver cloche. A hint of warm tomato sauce reached her nose and her stomach growled in anticipation.

"I'm sorry, Dad, but the food just arrived, and I haven't eaten all day."

"Go," he said. "I'll tell your mother you're fine the next time she wakes up."

"Call me if you hear anything," Hilary responded. "Even if it's the middle of the night, I want to know the second you have news about Jeff."

"I will, sweetie," he said. "Get some rest."

"You, too." Her father had to be exhausted as well. She knew he was likely trying to be strong and hold it together for her mother, which was its own kind of work. Hopefully he could get some sleep tonight.

Hilary ended the call and walked to the table. The

employee pulled out her chair and she sat, thanking him quietly. Then he removed the cloche, revealing pizza.

"Thank you," Oliver said. "That will be all for now."

"Please call when you're done," the young man said. "I will be happy to remove the dishes."

Hilary watched him leave, trying to adjust to the fact that she wasn't the one doing the serving for a change. It felt strange to be sitting here while someone else brought her food. Based on Oliver's expression, this was the norm for him.

He gestured to the salad with a questioning look and she nodded, handing him her plate. "I know the doctor said you should stick to light meals," he said as he placed the lettuce on her plate. "But I'd like to see you eat something, since I know you haven't had food other than that toast in the hospital."

"Believe me, I'm ready."

Oliver set her plate in front of her, and Hilary dug in, forgoing her usual manners. After a moment, she realized Oliver hadn't started yet and she glanced over to find him watching her, a smile playing at the corners of his mouth.

"I'm sorry," she mumbled.

"Don't be," he replied. "I'm not the queen. No need to stand on ceremony with me."

Hilary reached for a slice of pizza. "Do you do this a lot?"

He gave her a puzzled look as he forked a bite of salad. "Do what?"

She gestured to the room at large. "Eat in fancy hotel rooms while staff hovers nearby."

Oliver shook his head as he chewed. "Would it surprise you if I said the answer is no?"

She felt her eyebrows go up. "Actually, yes. I figured since you travel a lot, you must spend most of your time in hotels."

"I do," he said. "But I also have to attend a lot of business dinners and fundraisers."

It sounded glamorous, a far cry from her life of working at the restaurant and coming home to a microwavable dinner or a hastily prepared sandwich. Between her job and school, Hilary ate to live, not out of any enjoyment.

As if he'd read her mind, he continued. "It's not as nice as it sounds. I enjoy my job, but every time I'm at a gala or with colleagues, I always have to be on, you know? I can't really relax and just be myself for fear of offending someone or messing up a deal."

"That makes sense," Hilary said. "I can relate to that. As a server, I have to always be polite. No matter what a customer might say to me, I have to remain calm and respectful."

"Exactly!" Oliver leaned back in his chair a bit. "It's not like I want to turn into an asshole or anything. But laughing at lame jokes and pretending to be interested in someone's boring hobby gets old after a while. And don't get me started on the number of times I've had to swallow my pride and soothe someone's ego to get a deal to go through."

"Is it worth it?" She'd gotten a rough sense of Oliver's business activities from their conversations when he'd been in town. But he'd always swiftly redirected things, claiming he didn't want to bore her, or that he didn't want to talk business while he was on a break.

He took a sip of water before answering. "I think so," he finally said. "Most of my deals involve raising money for environmentally friendly companies or technologies. When I left after my last visit, I went to Malaysia to help broker a deal to build an offshore wind farm. They've already started construction, and once it's complete, it will help meet the growing power demand of the country without them needing to rely on fossil fuels. So I do think my work has value."

Hilary pondered his words while she ate. Oliver had cultivated a bit of a devil-may-care image, at least here in Blue Larkspur. She'd always suspected his charming attitude hid a depth of character, and now he'd given her a glimpse behind the curtain that proved her instincts were correct.

"Sounds like you're a bit of a crusader," she teased.

He flashed her a grin between bites of pizza. "I like to think of myself as a bit like a corporate Robin Hood. I don't steal from people, but I do my best to convince rich corporations and wealthy donors to part with their money. Then I give it to smaller countries or companies to fund environmental projects that will provide short- and long-term benefits."

"Did you always have an interest in the environment?" Hilary hadn't known him while she was growing up, so the finer details of Oliver's childhood were still a bit mysterious. He'd shared bits and pieces with her before, but there was a lot she didn't know.

He shook his head. "No. I messed around a lot as a teenager. I've told you a bit about that before."

"Yeah, I remember some of your stories." She chuckled. "You're lucky you made it out of some of those situations with all your parts intact."

"Don't I know it," he muttered darkly. "Thank God for Dom and Ezra. Those two knuckleheads never gave up on me, even when I was at my worst. If it wasn't for them, I wouldn't be where I am today."

"What do you think would have happened to you?"

Oliver's eyes seemed to lose focus as he stared into the middle distance. "Nothing good," he said quietly. "To be honest, I'd probably either be dead or in prison."

A chill ran over Hilary's skin. Given the things he'd told her, she'd assumed he was a bit of a juvenile delinquent, but just in a "kids will be kids" kind of way. Based on his response, though, it sounded like he hadn't told her everything about his past.

She cleared her throat. "Were things that bad?"

she asked lightly. What had he done that made him think he'd been on such a dark path? The Oliver she knew was funny, smart and kind. Had he really changed that much since his teenage years?

He looked at her again, seeming to pick up on her concern. "I never hurt anyone, if that's what you're worried about."

Hilary nodded, feeling better. Oliver had never shown any hint of violence, but it was becoming increasingly clear that she didn't really know him at all.

"I stole a few things, starting drinking. Probably would have experimented with drugs, if my brothers hadn't stepped in. Ezra had recently joined the army, and he threatened to hog-tie me and take my ass to basic training with him. Said they could get me enlisted once I showed up with him. And Dom was already making plans to attend the FBI academy. He told me if I didn't straighten up, he'd arrest me himself."

Hilary couldn't hide her smile. "It sounds like they love you very much."

"I know that now," Oliver said dryly. "But at the time I wasn't very happy with them. They weren't the only ones nagging me. My other siblings joined in whenever I saw them. Eventually, I realized I'd rather change than have to listen to them harp at me for the rest of my life."

Hilary pretended to write something down. "So what you're telling me is that if I prod you to change the baby's diaper long enough, you'll eventually do it without being asked?"

Oliver laughed, a rich, deep sound that washed over her and left her feeling warm inside. "You won't have to do that," he said. "I'm not going to shirk my duties on that front."

His words eased some of her deep-seated worries. "Does that mean you're going to be here?" She held her breath while she waited for him to answer the question. Given Oliver's lifestyle, she hadn't expected him to be around all that much, even after the baby was born. Maybe she didn't give him enough credit, but she'd figured his support would be more financial than physical. But given his remark about the diapers, perhaps she was wrong?

Oliver set down his fork and met her gaze. "I want to be a part of this baby's life." His tone was low and serious. "I'm not going to force myself into your life, but I want to be a real parent to our child. That means helping with feeding, diaper changes, baths, you name it."

Something inside her relaxed as his words sank in. Maybe Oliver's past troubles made him determined to redeem himself now that he was going to be a father? Hilary wasn't totally convinced of his words; after all, it was one thing to make promises and quite another to follow through, especially when that meant Oliver would have to make big changes in his life.

But it was a start. Something they could build on.

Hilary smiled. "I'm glad you said that. I do want this baby to have a father. But you should know that

I'm not going to make you do anything. If you're in, it's because you want to be. I'd rather do this alone than have you grow to resent our baby because of all the changes you'll have to make to be part of their life. As far as I'm concerned, no father is preferable to a bad one."

Oliver nodded. "I agree. Believe it or not, I had a dad who cared growing up. He made some terrible choices in his professional life, though, which changed everything. But before he died, he supported us and was there for us when we needed him. I plan on doing the same for this one."

Oh, how she hoped that was true! Before she could reply, Oliver's phone started to ring.

He pulled it from his pocket with a frown. "Excuse me, please. I need to take this."

He got to his feet and walked back into the living room, leaving her alone to finish her pizza.

Hilary chewed the last of her meal, listening to the low hum of his voice in the other room. Oliver was certainly saying all the things she wanted to hear at the moment. And hopefully, she could trust him to follow through.

As much as she wanted to believe him, a small part of her remained doubtful. It was almost as though she couldn't let herself fully trust him out of a sense of self-preservation. If she jumped in with both feet and he let her down, she'd be crushed. But if she held back, even a little bit, she wouldn't be destroyed if he decided the life of a doting dad wasn't for him.

But there was nothing she could do now. Only time would tell if Oliver was going to keep his word. And while she hated the sense of uncertainty, this was one area of her life where she was going to have to learn to accept it.

Chapter 8

Oliver hated to leave Hilary, as it felt like they were starting to get somewhere. But as soon as he'd seen Philip's name on his phone, he'd known he couldn't ignore the call.

"Hey," he said. "Please tell me you have good news?"

"I'm afraid not," Philip sighed. "BLPD is being stingy with information. As best as I can tell, they're treating it like a random crime. Jeff doesn't have a criminal record. His parents swear up and down their son wasn't in any trouble and they have no idea who would want to take him. Because the security cameras inside the restaurant were switched off, there isn't much to go on. I can keep digging, but you should know I'm getting significant push-back and I don't know how much more I'll be able to find for you."

"Don't worry about it," Oliver said. "The last thing I want is for you to get in trouble for trying to help. I appreciate what you've done."

"No problem," Philip assured him. "I'll keep my ear to the ground and let you know if I hear anything else."

"Thanks, man." Oliver ended the call and walked back to the table to rejoin Hilary.

"That was Philip Rees," he explained. "He's a detective in Boulder, and I asked him to do a little digging and see if he could learn anything about your brother's case."

"Did he find something?" Oliver heard the note of hope in Hilary's voice and his heart sank. He was going to have to disappoint her.

"I'm afraid not," he said gently.

She visibly deflated, her shoulders slumping slightly. "Figures," she muttered. "The police probably don't have a lot of clues."

"That's part of it," Oliver said. "And the fact that your parents can't think of anyone who would want to hurt or take your brother." Parents didn't know everything, though—had Jeff talked to Hilary about his problems? She'd told the police she didn't know anything when giving her statement in the hospital, but perhaps now she had remembered something?

"Do you have any idea who might have had an issue with your brother?"

She shook her head, frowning. "I don't. Jeff's gotten into trouble before, but nothing like this. He has seemed off lately, but he refused to talk to me about it. So I don't know anything."

He could tell how much this frustrated her and reached over to cover her hand with his. "None of this is your fault, and it's not your job to find your brother. Don't blame yourself for what's going on."

"I wish it was that easy," she said softly.

The chime of his phone interrupted them. This time, rather than step away, Oliver kept his hand on Hilary's and took the call at the table.

"What's up, Dom?"

"I've been looking into that case," his brother replied. "The news isn't great."

Hilary's eyes widened and Oliver put the call on speakerphone so she wouldn't have to strain to hear. "What did you find?"

"Jeff Weston has a gambling problem."

Hilary sucked in a breath but didn't speak.

"A big one," Dom continued. "He's currently in deep with a loan shark by the name of Vince Doherty."

"How deep?" Oliver asked. If the amount wasn't too outlandish, he might be able to help...

"Fifty thousand, as best I can tell," replied Dom.

Oliver whistled. Hilary's face lost all color and for a second, Oliver feared she might faint.

"Yeah," said Dom. "I think we're dealing with a ransom case here."

"Is the FBI involved yet?"

"No. Until BLPD asks for assistance, we can't do anything."

"His parents insist it's a random crime," Oliver told him. He briefly recapped what he'd just learned from Philip.

"That's pretty common," Dom said. "A lot of times, families are scared to involve law enforcement because the kidnapper threatens to harm or kill the family member who was taken. Wouldn't surprise me if that's what is going on here."

Oliver glanced at Hilary. "Maybe we can talk the parents into sharing the truth with the police."

"Wouldn't hurt to try."

Oliver thanked Dom and ended the call. Then he looked at Hilary.

She was still pale, but she no longer looked like she was about to pass out. There was a haunted look in her eyes, and he could tell his brother's information had deeply upset her.

For a split second, he regretted putting the call on speaker. Between the baby and the attack, she was stressed enough. But he didn't want her to think he was withholding information about her brother. Better for her to hear all of it. He could help her deal with the fallout.

"You seem surprised." Based on her reaction, it

was a safe bet she hadn't known about the gambling debts.

She shook her head, as though trying to make sense of it all. "Jeff has always enjoyed playing cards," she said slowly. "But I thought he knew better than to get in trouble like this. How does that even happen?" she looked at Oliver, her gaze questioning. "Why didn't he stop before things got too bad?"

Oliver shrugged. "It sounds like he might be a gambling addict. If that's the case, he probably *couldn't* stop. He knew the debt was mounting, but he likely figured one more hand would bring back his luck and turn things around. So things kept building and building until it was out of control."

"It's hard to believe," she said. "Are you sure your brother's sources are good? I mean, if Jeff's problems were this big, I would have heard about it."

"From your parents?" Oliver asked. She nodded, so he decided to push a little. "You really think they'd tell you about your brother's gambling?"

Her shoulders stiffened slightly. "Why wouldn't they?"

"To protect you," he replied. "Fifty thousand is a massive amount of debt. It's likely your brother is ashamed and doesn't want anyone to know. He probably swore them to secrecy. Besides, I bet your parents would want to keep that information from you, so you don't feel obligated to help him."

Hilary opened her mouth, then closed it. "That

does sound like something they would do," she acknowledged grudgingly.

Oliver squeezed her hand. "Your first instinct is to help people," he said softly. "It's one of your best qualities. But it also puts you at risk. There are people out there who would take advantage of your generosity. I bet your parents know this and wanted to keep you out of it. For your brother's sake, and your own."

"I have to call them." There was an urgency in her voice Oliver hadn't heard before. "I need to know if it's true."

Her hands shook as she retrieved her phone and punched in the number. Oliver wanted to hold her, to kiss her, to soothe away her worries, but there was a brittle air about her that gave him pause. Unless he missed his guess, Hilary was barely holding it together. She might welcome his embrace, but it was equally likely she'd shove him away and reject his attempt to comfort her. Not wanting to jeopardize the tenuous progress they'd made, he kept his hands to himself.

Hilary placed the phone flat on the table and put the call on speaker. It was a small gesture, but one he appreciated. The fact that she wanted to include him in her family's business made him feel like she valued his opinion.

"Hilary?" Her dad answered the phone, his concern clear in his voice. "Is everything all right, honey?"

"I heard something about Jeff," she said, her tone flat. "Is it true?"

"Is what true?" Greg Weston's frown came over the line as he evidently tried to decipher what his daughter was asking.

"Jeff has been gambling. A lot," Hilary added for emphasis. "Did you know about his debts?"

Her father didn't answer right away. As the silence stretched, Oliver's suspicions were confirmed.

"Why didn't you tell me?" Hilary's voice wavered as her emotion started to bleed through her earlier composure.

The resulting sigh was heavy, full of secrets and things left unsaid. "We didn't want you to worry."

"So you did know." Hilary shook her head, her eyes bright with tears. "What about Mom?"

"Yes," her father admitted. "We came up with a plan to help your brother pay off his debts. But it looks like his creditor got tired of waiting."

"Just what were you going to do?" Her voice rose as she spoke, her tone intensifying. "How did you and Mom think you were going to save him this time?"

"The restaurant." Her father sounded tired. "We've put it up for sale."

Hilary's mouth dropped open in shock. Oliver reached for her hand, but she pulled away before he could touch her.

She was very still as she spoke again. "The restaurant is your livelihood. How will you and Mom survive if you sell it to pay off Jeff's gambling debts?"

"We'll figure something out," he replied. "But we have to do something! We can't just leave your brother out there—God only knows what they'll do to him if we don't pay!"

"And what about next time?" Hilary asked. "Jeff isn't going to stop, not in the long term. What are you going to sell the next time he racks up a huge debt? Are you and Mom going to live on the street?"

"It won't come to that," her dad insisted. Hilary shook her head again, and Oliver found himself silently agreeing with her. If her parents bailed him out, Jeff might straighten up for a bit but sooner or later he'd go back to his old ways. And the next time, his parents probably wouldn't be able to raise the cash to save him.

"You need to go to the police," Hilary said. "You have to come clean with them. Otherwise, they're wasting time when they could be actually finding Jeff."

"No." Her father started speaking over her before she'd finished. "The instructions are very clear. If we go to the police or involve any kind of investigator, they'll torture your brother and kill him." He paused to draw a shaky breath. "I can't let that happen, do you understand? I'd never forgive myself if…" He trailed off with a sniff.

"When is the deadline to pay?" Hilary's voice was gentle now, an acknowledgment of her father's pain.

"Friday." He sounded defeated, as though he knew nearly a week wasn't going to be enough time.

"Dad…" She hesitated, apparently recognizing the futility of the situation as well. She met Oliver's gaze, her expression distraught. A sense of helplessness filled him; he wished he could do something, anything, to help her.

"I know." Hilary's father was silent for a few seconds. "Someone will buy Atria," he continued. "I have to believe that."

"And if they don't?" She spoke so softly, Oliver wasn't certain her father heard the question.

"Just focus on feeling better," the older man said. "Let me and your mother worry about Jeff. We'll get him back."

Oliver didn't have the heart to disagree, at least not out loud. It was clear Hilary's parents were deep in denial and pointing that out wasn't going to help the situation. He remained silent while she ended the call, wanting to give her a moment to process everything.

She sat still for a moment, staring at the phone on the table. He could tell by the look on her face that she was having trouble accepting the news that her parents not only knew about her brother's debt but were planning to sell the restaurant to pay his ransom.

"Hilary," he said quietly. "Are you okay?" She looked broken, as if she'd been beaten down by life. He wanted desperately to help her, but what could he do? It wasn't as though he had a magic wand he could wave to suddenly release her brother.

"Do you want to talk about it?" At least he could listen to her worries and fears. He might not be able to fix them, but he could lend a shoulder for her to cry on, if she needed it.

"I…" She cleared her throat, then spoke again. "I'm going to bed."

"Oh." He didn't want to argue with her; he knew she must still be tired, and he wasn't about to suggest she skip an opportunity to rest. But he hated the idea of her going to sleep while she was still upset.

She got to her feet and he quickly followed suit. "If you need anything, I'm here."

Hilary offered him a small smile. "I know. Thank you."

Then she was gone, leaving him alone with the empty dishes.

She couldn't sleep.

Maybe it was the nap she'd taken earlier, messing with her sleep schedule?

Maybe it was the aftermath of her head injury and the shock of finding out she was pregnant?

Or maybe it was finding out that her irresponsible brother had racked up tens of thousands of dollars in gambling debts and her parents were trying to sell their livelihood to pay his ransom so he would be returned to the family?

At this point, Hilary was so angry with Jeff that she wasn't sure she even wanted him back.

How could he have done this? Yeah, he'd always liked playing cards, but he'd never been so reckless before. He'd owed money, but not on a scale like this!

Why hadn't he stopped playing? Once the debt started mounting, he should have quit before things got worse. Instead, he'd plowed ahead, digging an even bigger hole for himself.

And now her parents were involved.

Atria was their life's work, a dream fulfilled for the both of them. Her mom and dad had built the restaurant from a small café, gradually expanding to become one of Blue Larkspur's favorite destinations. The place had hosted countless parties, marriage proposals, retirement dinners. It was a staple in the community, with so many people making memories and celebrating special moments at one of its tables.

Hilary couldn't remember a time without Atria in her life. As a child, she'd done her homework at a small table in a corner of the kitchen. As she'd grown, she'd helped wash dishes, roll silverware, organize menus. Eventually, she'd graduated to waitressing and front of house management while Jeff took a different path and focused on becoming a chef. Under his management, the menu had expanded, drawing the attention of food critics and expanding their clientele. Now, it wasn't unheard of for people to drive in from out of town to enjoy a meal at Atria.

The success of the restaurant made Hilary proud, not only of her work, but the efforts of her family. They'd truly been a team, each one with a part to play. And up until now, Hilary had thought she and her parents and her brother had shared a common goal: to continue making Atria the best it could be.

Now? She realized Jeff's addiction—and that's exactly what it was—had put all of their hard work in jeopardy.

The thought of her parents selling Atria broke her heart. What would her mom and dad do if they didn't have the restaurant to go to every day? They loved that place so much—the running Weston family joke was that Atria was their third child. They were there every day, even if the place was closed. They always found something to do, from cleaning an already clean counter, to painting over a subtle smudge left behind by a customer bumping a chair into the wall. Their lives were Atria. If that was taken away, what would become of them?

There had to be another way. Surely there was an option they hadn't considered, a possibility left unexplored? But even as she had the thought, she realized there wasn't. Her own savings were no match for Jeff's debt. She knew her parents were likely in the same boat. They made enough from the restaurant to survive, but most of the profits were rolled back into the place, paying for staff salaries, supplies and upkeep. If they raised prices the customers would walk. Besides, that approach wouldn't generate the money fast enough to pay Jeff's ransom.

It seemed her dad was right. Short of winning the lottery, the only way to get the funds to settle Jeff's account was to sell Atria.

A shiver went down her spine as the implications of this action set in. Hilary made enough from waitressing to support herself and pay for school. What if the new owners decided to bring in all new staff? Even if they kept most of the employees, it was unlikely they would want her around, seeing as how she was the daughter of the former owners. Her job was in jeopardy, and with it, her ability to provide for herself and her baby.

There were other restaurants in Blue Larkspur, but who would want to hire a pregnant waitress who had plans on leaving as soon as she finished her degree? As her pregnancy became more advanced, Hilary would have a harder time being on her feet all day. She was going to have to find another job, one that would allow her to sit some throughout her workday.

Oliver's face flashed in her mind. He'd said something about helping her, even before he knew he was the baby's father. She could swallow her pride and ask him for money to provide for them, but she'd rather starve than ask him to support her. Her pride simply wouldn't allow it. And now that she knew her parents were selling Atria to bail out Jeff, she couldn't very well ask them for help if necessary.

No, she was going to have to figure something out, and the sooner the better.

Her future, and her baby's future, depended on it.

Chapter 9

Monday

"I want to help."

He'd meant to say good morning first or ask her how she'd slept. But after taking a moment to enjoy the sight of her sleep-mussed hair, the words tumbled out before he could think twice.

Hilary blinked at him, clearly taken aback. "Uh, what?"

"Your brother," Oliver clarified. "I want to help get your brother back."

He'd spent a good part of the night brainstorming ways to help Hilary's family solve this particular problem. He'd seen the look on her face when her father had mentioned selling the restaurant—she'd been shocked. But more than that, it had seemed like something had broken inside of her.

He couldn't very well stand there and do nothing while Hilary dealt with the aftermath of her brother's bad choices. That kind of stress would be bad for her.

And the baby, of course.

So he'd decided to do something about it.

If she would let him, that is…

He followed her to the table and watched as she poured herself a cup of coffee from the silver pot the staff had brought up shortly before she'd emerged from the bedroom. She was beautiful, her hair slightly tousled in the morning light. He had the sudden urge to reach for her, to feel the warmth of sleep that must still be on her skin.

Instead, he forced himself to speak.

"I have an idea that might work."

Hilary held up a hand. He waited while she took a sip.

After a few seconds, she sighed quietly. "Okay, now I'm awake."

Oliver smiled. "Sorry, I forgot you might need coffee."

"It's okay, I had some trouble falling asleep last night, so I'm moving a little slowly this morning."

"Was the bed uncomfortable?" He began to reach for the phone to call housekeeping. Maybe they could bring up some extra pillows or blankets for her?

"No, not at all," she replied, stalling his movement. "The bed was great. The room was perfect. I just couldn't turn off my brain."

He nodded, relating all too well to what she was saying. "I think I can help with that."

She sat at the table, her hands wrapped around the mug. "What's going on?"

"Your parents shouldn't have to sell the restaurant." Based on Hilary's reaction last night, he knew Atria was more than just a business to her. It stood to reason her parents felt the same way.

She sighed and glanced away. "No, I'm pretty sure they do. I went over and over different ideas last night, but I couldn't come up with another way to raise fifty thousand dollars in such a short period of time. Dad texted me last night and said they already had an offer. I think they have to accept it."

"You could ask me," he said simply.

Hilary gaped at him, then set the coffee cup on the table with a soft *thunk*. "No." She shook her head for emphasis. "I can't do that."

Oliver pulled out the chair across from her and sat down, then placed his forearms on the table and linked his hands. He'd anticipated this reaction, planned for it. "Okay, fine," he said agreeably. "You don't have to ask. I'm offering."

"No." Hilary's tone was flat. "That's out of the question."

He tilted his head to the side. "Why? Don't you want to get your brother back?"

"Only so I can kill him myself," she muttered

darkly. Oliver couldn't help but laugh at the unexpected response. Hilary looked at him, one eyebrow raised. "You think I'm joking? It would be one thing if his actions affected only himself. But Jeff's gambling is going to cost my family their business, has put my parents under a lot of stress and has left me with stitches in the back of my head and a hospital bill. It's not okay."

"I didn't say it was," Oliver replied. "And you can certainly bring all of that up with him when you see him again. But that's not going to happen unless his ransom is paid."

Hilary looked down, her anger seeming to fade. "I know," she said softly.

"So let me help." He ducked his head, trying to catch her eye. "I want to get your brother back, and I'm able to do it. There's no need to make this harder on your family than it has to be."

"You don't need to get involved." She glanced up, her eyebrows drawn together in worry. "I appreciate the offer, but I can't let you do that."

Exasperation began to rise in Oliver's chest. "Give me a reason why," he said. "What's so wrong about me stepping in?"

Hilary pushed her coffee cup away and crossed her arms. "If it wasn't for you finding me last night, you wouldn't be involved in this."

She paused, so he pushed her. "Yes, and?"

"The only reason you're still here is because of the baby." It sounded like she was forcing the words out, pushing them through clenched teeth. "It's okay if you want to help support the baby. But I'm not going to let you take care of my family. We're not a charity case."

Oliver slowly sat back, awareness dawning. Hilary had said "we're not a charity case," but he could read between the lines. She'd actually meant "I'm." Her ego wouldn't allow her to accept help from him, even if it meant losing the family business.

He'd known this was a possibility, but he hadn't thought Hilary would be so stubborn as to let her pride take over when she was in dire straits.

"I see," he said slowly. "What if I framed this a different way? Don't think of it as a donation. Consider it a loan. Jeff and I will come up with a contract and payment schedule, so he can pay me back over time."

"And if he defaults?" Her voice was heavy with skepticism; apparently, Hilary's opinion of her brother couldn't get much lower.

"If he does, it will be my problem." In truth, Oliver didn't have high hopes of seeing the cash again. He'd always refrained from mixing money with friends and family, knowing that it was a recipe for disaster. This was a special case, though, and he was going to have to make an exception. Fortunately, he could afford to lose the funds, especially since it would take a major source of strain away from Hilary and, by default, the baby.

Hilary still didn't look convinced. "Look," he

said, leaning forward again. "The priority right now has to be getting Jeff back. Once we do that, we can figure out everything else. A payment plan, getting him help for his addiction, moving forward. I know you want to get all the details resolved now, but until we actually talk to your brother, that's not going to happen."

She sighed, studying his face with troubled eyes. "Why are you doing this?" She seemed genuinely confused, as though she didn't understand why he was choosing to get involved in her family's problems.

Taking a chance, Oliver reached across the table and took her hand. "Because I care about you, and I see how this is weighing on you. Like it or not, this baby means we're connected for the rest of our lives. That means I'm tied to your family now, as well as my own. Paying your brother's ransom helps your family, and it helps the baby, too."

Hilary flipped her hand over, curling her fingers to link with his. "Are you sure?" Her voice was barely above a whisper, as if she was afraid the answer might be no.

"I'm absolutely sure," he told her.

"I don't know how to thank you." She blinked, her eyes shiny with unshed tears.

"You just did." He took a deep breath, knowing he had to handle this next part carefully. "I'm doing this because I want to help your family. I'm not stepping in to be a hero, or so that you or your family will feel indebted to me. I want you to understand that."

Hilary reached for her coffee cup and took a careful sip. "All right," she said finally. "I believe you. But it's going to be hard to convince my mother not to overreact. I'm sure you're going to get free food for life, and she'll load you up with meals every time she sees you."

Oliver laughed. "I wouldn't say no to the occasional plate. But in all seriousness, as far as I'm concerned, this arrangement is between myself and Jeff. There's no need for you or your parents to involve yourselves or worry about if he is or isn't paying me back."

Hilary pressed her lips together, clearly wanting to say something. Instead, she settled for a nod. "Can I make one request?"

Oliver tilted his head to the side. "Sure. What is it?"

She sighed quietly. "I don't want this to happen again. I know Jeff is an adult, and you can't force someone to do something they don't want, but…"

"But?" Oliver prodded.

Hilary traced the rim of her cup with her forefinger. "I think he needs treatment for his gambling addiction. And I think once he's released, he'll be shaken by this experience and more likely to seek treatment. The more time that passes, the more likely his fear will fade and his denial about his addiction will take over."

"You're probably right." Oliver knew from experience that denial was a powerful force, one that had ruled his life for too long. If Ezra and Dom hadn't hounded him about his own mistakes, he wouldn't be where he was today.

Would Jeff be receptive to an intervention? Hopefully being kidnapped would strike fear into his heart and help him realize things had to change. But if he remained stubborn, no amount of begging or pleading would affect him.

Hilary went on, "I just think that if you told him he has to go to treatment as part of your deal, he probably would. Otherwise, he'll go right back to his old ways."

Oliver nodded, struck by Hilary's obvious concern for her brother. Even though Jeff's actions had put a severe strain on her family, and despite her justified anger toward him, she still wanted the best for him. Not many people were able to keep their emotions from clouding their judgment, especially when money was involved. A smile formed at the corners of his mouth; he was glad he didn't have to face her in a corporate setting. She'd make a formidable opponent in the boardroom.

Hilary noticed his expression and narrowed her eyes. "What's so funny?"

"Nothing," he said. "I was just thinking about what a good negotiator you'd make. If you're ever looking for a career change, I know several companies who would be thrilled to add you to their team."

He'd almost offered to hire her himself but refrained at the last moment. Hilary was a proud woman, and he knew she was having a hard time accepting his offer to bail out her brother. The last thing he wanted was to appear condescending, as if he was offering her a job out of a sense of obligation.

Besides, while working together might be enjoyable in the short term, it had the potential to complicate matters in the long run.

Hilary laughed. "You corporate types forget how much skill it takes to work in a customer-facing role. Patience, tact, diplomacy—they're not just important for the C-suite."

She was right, and it humbled him to realize he'd overlooked those aspects of her job. "That's true," he acknowledged. "Sometimes I forget how much you have to deal with on a daily basis."

Hilary blinked, clearly taken aback. "You're not the only one," she said. "I've had professors who are shocked by some of the things I talk about in my papers. They have a hard time believing a waitress has practical experience with some of the ideas presented in class."

"Like what?" Oliver knew she was working on her master's degree in international marketing but wasn't familiar with what the coursework would entail.

She shrugged. "Some of my classes focused on consumer behavior in a free market system. I was able to pull examples from the restaurant to talk about how menu design appears to influence customer choice. My parents even let me try a few experiments, where I changed the menu description for a few dishes and recorded how that affected ordering frequency."

"That sounds interesting." He was genuinely impressed by her creativity and the way she was blending work and school.

She waved her hand, brushing aside the compliment. "Thanks. It was a good class and I enjoyed it."

"It sounds like you've found your calling."

She offered him a small smile. "I hope so. But I'm not sure how that's going to go now." She looked down, referencing her belly.

"You're going to finish school," Oliver said firmly. "If that's what you want to do. I'll take care of the baby so you can study as much as you need to." The weight of responsibility that had settled over him as soon as he'd learned the child was his grew a little bit heavier. It wasn't just the little one who would be affected by his choices now—Hilary's life and future career would be affected, too.

Oliver knew he wouldn't be able to live with himself if Hilary had to give up her dreams because he wasn't pulling his weight, parenting-wise. Not to mention, if she had to quit school she'd likely end up resenting him over time, which would make it harder for them to effectively co-parent. He couldn't let that happen—not if there was something he could do to prevent it. He wasn't going to let her down the way his father had let down his family.

"I do want to keep going," she said. "If there's a way to make it work." She shrugged. "But that's something to worry about later. Right now, we need to get Jeff back."

Oliver nodded, accepting her change of topic. "I know the kidnappers told your parents they had until Friday to come up with the funds, but I see no reason to wait. The sooner we pay, the sooner Jeff is released, hopefully unharmed."

"Okay." Hilary finished her coffee and stood. "Give me a few minutes to get dressed. Then we can go see my parents. They might be able to tell us how to get in touch with the kidnappers."

He watched her walk away, his admiration for her strength growing the more time they spent together. He'd always found her attractive, but now he was seeing layers and depth to Hilary that he'd never noticed before.

Thinking back to some of his past relationships, he felt a quick burst of relief at the fact that she was the one carrying his child, rather than one of his former girlfriends. If a surprise like this had to happen, at least his baby was going to have a mother he wanted to be around.

Hopefully she could say the same about him.

It didn't take her long to get ready.

Hilary didn't have an extensive morning routine and she cut a few corners today to save time. That meant no makeup, and her hair thrown back in a ponytail. A few months ago, she would have cringed at the thought of being around Oliver without looking her best, but after the events of the past twenty-four hours her priorities had shifted.

Now she stared out the window of the car, watching the familiar sights of Blue Larkspur pass by without really seeing them. She still couldn't believe Oliver was going to pay Jeff's ransom—she'd known he was well-off, but the fact that he apparently thought nothing of shelling out that kind of money for someone he'd never met made her realize he was richer than she'd initially imagined.

His gesture had made her feel simultaneously relieved and unsettled. Even though Oliver had insisted he was making a deal with her brother, she still felt beholden to him. Without his generosity, her parents would have had to sell Atria, and who knows if they would have been able to raise the funds in time?

A small voice in her head wondered at Oliver's true motivations. He'd said he wanted to take the stress off of her, for the baby's sake. It sounded sweet, but what if there was more to it than that? What if Oliver was going to use this as a way to exert control over her and later, their child?

He'd never seemed particularly controlling before, but now that he was going to be a father, maybe that would change?

She glanced at him out of the corner of her eye. He appeared relaxed, totally at ease as he drove them through Blue Larkspur. Did the man ever get flustered? He always projected an air of calm confidence, as though he was prepared to handle anything that might come his way.

Paying a ransom to get his baby mama's brother back? No problem.

Alien invasion? Just another day at the office.

What is that like? she wondered. More importantly, how could she develop that attitude for herself? Because right now, she was feeling all kinds of stressed.

"It's going to be okay." His deep voice broke the silence and cut through her thoughts.

Was he a mind reader now, too? "I know," she said, sounding a little defensive even to herself.

His hand came over hers, large and warm and comforting. "I can feel the tension coming off your body. It can't be good for you."

"Because of the baby, right?" Hilary didn't mean to lash out, but more and more, it felt like Oliver only cared about the pregnancy. While she was glad he was interested and had plans to be an involved father, she was more than just a vessel for his child. If people were going to spend the next months treating her like spun glass, she might not make it through this experience with her sanity intact.

To her surprise, Oliver yanked the steering wheel to the right and made a sharp turn into an empty parking lot. He shifted the car into Park, then unbuckled his seat belt and turned to fully face her.

Hilary's heart thumped hard against her chest as

he stared at her, his blue eyes bright with emotion. She released her seat belt and shifted a bit, putting a little more distance between them. She'd never seen him like this before, and it worried her.

"Let's get something straight." He raked a hand through his hair, mussing the strands slightly. "I care about this baby, absolutely. But right now, it's still an abstract concept to me, not someone I know. You, on the other hand, I do know. And my feelings for you are separate from the pregnancy."

Hilary blinked, taking in his words. "They are?"

His laugh was harsh, without its usual warmth. "Of course. I thought I had made that clear."

"I know you want us to be friends—"

"No." He shook his head, interrupting her. "I don't want to be your friend." He put a strange emphasis on the word *friend*, but before she could decipher what that meant, Oliver muttered a curse.

Between one breath and the next, he moved, reaching for her. One hand cupped the side of her face, while the other landed on her shoulder. Then he lunged forward and captured her mouth with his.

His lips were firm and warm, slanting over hers perfectly. Hilary held her breath, too surprised by the contact to do much more than freeze. But after a few seconds, she relaxed against him, darting her tongue out to taste him.

Oliver deepened the kiss, pulling her against him. Her breasts flattened against the solid wall of his chest, sending delicious shivers of sensation to her core. He was strong and big and safe, his embrace powerful yet gentle. And oh, how much she'd missed him!

She wasn't sure how long the kiss lasted—it might have been only seconds, but it felt like a moment out of time. For one magical instant, all her worries and troubles disappeared. The only thing that mattered was Oliver and the feel of his lips and tongue and hands, the scent of him filling her head and the warmth of his body seeping into her skin.

All too soon, he pulled away. His breathing was ragged as he stared down at her, a look of surprise on his face as though he couldn't quite believe what had just happened.

With the loss of contact, Hilary's thoughts started up again. "I… I…" She tried to speak but couldn't figure out what to say.

"I'm sorry." He released her, leaning back into his own seat. He ran his palm over his mouth, like he was trying to wipe away the remains of her kiss.

"Why?" His apology stung, leaving her feeling unwanted. Apparently, he hadn't enjoyed their kiss as much as she had.

He glanced at her cautiously. "I shouldn't have grabbed you like that."

"It's okay," she said, straightening her shirt. "I'm just a little confused. You told me over and over that we're friends, but that…" she trailed off, shaking her head. "Friends don't kiss each other like that."

"No, they don't," he said quietly. Oliver looked down at his lap, clenching and unclenching his hands.

Hilary could have let him off the hook, pretended like nothing had happened. But Oliver's kiss had changed things, and she wasn't sure she wanted to go back to the way they were before.

"So which is it?" she asked. "Are we going to ignore this and pretend like we're just friends?"

Oliver sighed. "I think it's pretty clear that I want you. But after what you said at the restaurant the other night, I have no intention of forcing myself on you, or pressuring you for something you're not willing to give."

It struck her then that she was standing at a crossroads. Down one path, she and Oliver had a cordial relationship, one in which they ignored their feelings and kept things superficial for the sake of the baby. On the other path, they acknowledged this attraction and acted on it, taking a chance on romance.

The former was the safe, logical choice. The latter was riskier but had the potential for great rewards.

Hilary took a deep breath, her mind warring with her heart. She wanted Oliver—she always had. The one night with him hadn't been enough. Why couldn't she have both him and the baby? It wasn't going to be easy, but there was no good reason why they couldn't try to make things work.

Except…what if it didn't? Oliver had said before that they were tied to each other forever, thanks to their child. If a prospective relationship between them failed, would they still be able to put aside hurt feelings and do the right thing for their kid?

Hilary didn't know what the future held. But in this moment, she couldn't deny that she was willing to take a chance. Better to try and fail than never try at all.

"Oliver." Time to see if he felt the same way. "I told you I'd moved on because at the time, I didn't think you were going to stick around for long. I knew if I slept with you again, you'd break my heart when you left."

He looked over at her, his expression alert. "Oh?"

She nodded. "Can you blame me? You're usually only here for a few days, and it didn't seem like you were looking for anything more than a good time. But things are different now."

He chuckled softly. "That's certainly true."

"I want you, too," she continued. "And if you're interested, we can see where this goes."

He angled to face her again, his eyes practically glowing with desire.

And hope.

"Do you mean that?" He sounded almost shy. "You're not just saying that because I'm helping you?"

Hilary reached for his hand, lacing her fingers through his. He'd spent so much time reassuring her and now it was her chance to return the favor. "No. I appreciate what you're doing for my family, but my attraction for you has nothing to do with it."

His smile was slow and sensual. Her stomach did a little flip and the temperature inside the car seemed to rise a few degrees. "It means a lot to hear you say that. If we didn't have somewhere to be right now, I'd take you back to the hotel and show you just how much I've been hoping for this moment."

Hilary's growing arousal cooled at the reminder of her brother and the reason for their trip. "I have to say, selfishly, I hope it doesn't take long to get Jeff back. We have a lot to talk about and focus on right now, and I feel like I can't do that with Jeff's safety still uncertain."

Oliver squeezed her hand. "We'll get him back. In my experience, money has a way of opening doors. Once his kidnappers realize we're going to pay, they'll release him."

"I hope you're right." Hilary's imagination had no trouble conjuring up any number of scenarios where the kidnappers refused to let her brother go. What if they demanded more money? What if they decided to take the money but still hold him hostage? Worst of all, what if they took the money and killed Jeff?

Oliver turned back and refastened his seat belt. Hilary did the same, then he put the car in gear and steered them back onto the road. "Whatever happens, we'll face it together."

Hilary smiled, feeling like part of a team. With Oliver by her side, she was ready to face anything.

No matter what the future might hold.

Chapter 10

Oliver wasn't sure what to expect from Hilary's parents, so he decided to follow her lead.

She'd entered the house confidently, not even bothering to knock. "Mom? Dad? It's me."

Her father had walked out of the kitchen, drying his hands on a dish towel. The older man practically ran to her, genuine happiness and relief on his face. Then his eyes had filled with tears and he'd hugged her tightly, asking for forgiveness for leaving the cameras off.

Hilary had done an admirable job of soothing her dad's feelings, reassuring him that she was fine and would be okay. She'd introduced Oliver, and the man had sniffled and looked at him, apparently registering his presence for the first time.

"Of course," said Greg Weston. "My apologies. I remember you from the hospital. And I've seen you at Atria before." He glanced at his daughter. "Is he the one your mother told me you're staying with?"

Oliver shook his hand. "Yes. I have a large suite at the Metropolitan. She's staying in one of the guest bedrooms. The doctor didn't want her to be alone while she recovers."

Greg nodded. "Thank you. Cheryl and I are just so…" He trailed off, waving his hands. "We're at a loss," he finished. "Please, have a seat."

"Where is Mom?" Hilary asked.

"Still in bed," said her father. "I tried to get her to eat something for breakfast this morning, but she says she's not hungry. She took a few bites of toast to humor me, but I can't get her to leave the bedroom."

Hilary frowned. "Maybe I should go check on her." She glanced at Oliver, silently asking if he would be okay alone with her father. Oliver gave her a small smile and she left the room.

Greg seemed lost in thought, not really registering his daughter's departure. Oliver leaned forward, wondering how best to talk to the older man. It was clear he was almost at his breaking point, and no wonder. One child had been hospitalized, one was missing, his wife was inconsolable and he was facing the prospect of selling his restaurant. The fact that he was even functioning right now was admirable.

"Mr. Weston," Oliver began.

Greg's eyes swung to his and focused. "Yes?" He shook his head. "I'm sorry, where are my manners? Would you like something to drink? Water or coffee, perhaps?"

Oliver shook his head. "No, thank you. I wanted to talk to you about Jeff's situation."

"It's under control," the older man replied automatically. "We're taking care of it."

"Hilary told me your plan." He had to tread carefully here; it was clear Greg's first instinct was to appear in control. Oliver recognized the impulse—it was a tactic he often deployed when facing uncertainty. In his experience, if he faked being in control long enough, things usually worked themselves around until he actually was.

Of course, that was in business matters. Not when dealing with a kidnapping and ransom demand.

"We've had some inquiries from interested parties." Greg's gaze flitted around the room, landing here, then there. "There's a serious offer on the table now."

"And then what?"

Greg looked at him then, frowning. "What do you mean?"

"Let's assume you go through with the sale. Do you think you could get the paperwork drawn up and the deal finalized in time to pay Jeff's ransom?" Oliver didn't give Greg a chance to respond before continuing. "Even if that all works out, where does that leave you and Mrs. Weston? How will you make a living if Atria is gone?"

Greg shook his head and Oliver recognized the stubborn glint in his eyes. "I can't worry about that right now. I have to get my son back." He shot to his feet and began to pace, running his hand over his unshaven face. "You don't understand, Mr. Colton. You don't have children. But I'd do anything for my kids. Whatever it takes."

It was on the tip of Oliver's tongue to mention the baby, but he held back. Now was not the time. "I may have another solution for you. And please, call me Oliver." *I'm the father of your daughter's baby*, he thought. *So we might as well dispense with the formalities.*

Greg stopped pacing and looked at him, his expression simultaneously wary and hopeful. "What are you thinking?"

"I'm a venture capitalist," Oliver explained. "And I'm fortunate enough to have done very well in business. I want to pay Jeff's ransom."

Greg's jaw dropped and he sank onto his chair. "You what?"

"I've talked this over with Hilary," Oliver continued. "I'm going to pay Jeff's ransom. Once he's released, Jeff and I will work out a schedule so he can pay me back. But the priority right now is to get him released and into treatment for his gambling addiction."

"I don't understand." Greg's voice was weak. "Why would you do that? Do you even know Jeff?"

Oliver leaned forward, resting his elbows on his knees. "I don't know him, not yet anyway. But I do know Hilary, and I care about her very much. This experience has put a lot of strain on all of you, and I'm in a position to relieve it."

Greg shook his head, clearly having trouble believing what Oliver was telling him. "I don't know what to say."

"Just say yes," Oliver replied easily. "I'm prepared to do this today. Hilary and I came here so she could check on both of you, and so we could get the number for the kidnappers. I want to call and arrange the exchange."

Greg's face crumpled with despair. "I don't know the number. The man told me he'd contact me on Friday, and not to involve the cops. My phone didn't register anything—it said 'Restricted' when they called."

"Have you made other calls since you heard from them?" It didn't hurt to ask, though Oliver suspected he already knew the answer. If Greg hadn't used his phone again, Dom might be able to pull a number.

"Yes," Greg said. "Why, should I not have done that?"

"It's okay," Oliver said. No point in mentioning a trace now, especially since the older man didn't want the police involved.

"So does this mean we have to wait until Friday

to do anything?" Oliver heard the strain in Greg's voice and knew this had to be incredibly difficult for him. Oliver hadn't met his unborn child yet, but given Ezra's past in the army, he knew all too well what it was like to realize someone he loved was in danger and he would have to wait days before being able to do anything about it. Just the idea of having to worry about Hilary like that was enough to make his palms sweat.

"Maybe we'll get lucky and the kidnappers will call again," Oliver suggested. "If they do, tell them right away that you have the money."

"Are you really serious about this?" Greg's voice shook and he sounded like he was on the verge of tears.

"I am," Oliver said gently.

"He is," echoed Hilary from the doorway. She gave Oliver's shoulder a squeeze as she walked past him to sit next to her father. She reached over and placed her hand on his knee. "Oliver is a man of his word," she continued. "If he says he's going to do something, he'll do it."

Hearing Hilary voice her trust in him made Oliver feel ten feet tall. It touched him to know that she believed in him and accepted his help. It was like catnip for his ego.

Greg nodded, accepting her words. "How's your mother?" he asked.

Hilary sighed softly. "Depressed. She was happy to see me for a moment, but then she started crying about Jeff. I told her it was going to be okay, but I know she doesn't believe me. After a few minutes she said she was tired and asked me to go." She glanced at Oliver and he saw the worry in her eyes. The sooner Jeff was released, the better it would be for everyone.

"She'll be fine once your brother is back." Greg sounded confident, but Oliver suspected he was bluffing.

"Is there anything we can do in the meantime?" Hilary asked. "Food, company, anything at all?"

Greg smiled sadly and shook his head. "We're not hungry, and at this point, you've seen what terrible company we are. I just need you to keep recovering, and when the kidnappers call again on Friday we'll make arrangements. We just have to wait until then."

"You don't have their number?" Hilary looked at Oliver again for confirmation and he shook his head.

"It was blocked," he said. "Nothing showed up on your dad's caller ID."

Hilary's face fell. "Oh."

"They might make contact before Friday," Oliver pointed out, wanting to inject a little hope into the situation. He couldn't stand to see her looking so forlorn, and now that he knew his attraction to her was returned, he could offer to comfort her.

Just maybe not in front of her father.

"I hope so," she replied. She reached for his hand and he got to his feet and helped her to stand. He put his arm around her shoulders, tucking her close to his side.

Greg eyed the two of them as he rose, awareness dawning on his face. "Let me know if you need anything, sweetie." He nodded at Oliver. "I can't thank you enough for what you're doing."

"It's my pleasure," Oliver replied. It was the truth—helping Hilary triggered a feeling of satisfaction that he hadn't felt in quite some time. It was nice to have someone to care about like this, and he was glad he had the resources to make a difference in her life.

They walked out of her parents' house together and Oliver shortened his stride to match hers. He was disappointed not to have a number for the kidnappers, but at least her father knew what to tell them the next time they called.

He unlocked the car and opened the passenger door for Hilary, but instead of sitting down she stood frozen in place, staring at the rental with a slight frown.

"Is something wrong?" A spike of fear pricked him as his mind began to conjure up distressing possibilities. Was her head hurting again? Was something going on with the baby? Why wasn't she moving?

"Oliver." She said his name slowly, like she was thinking through something. "I think I might have a way to find the men who took Jeff." She looked up at him then, her eyes bright with excitement.

"What? How?" Unless he missed his guess, she

was remembering something from the attack. Would it be enough to lead them to her brother's kidnappers?

"A car," she replied. "I remember seeing a car cruising the parking lot several times over the last week. I never saw it stop—it would always slowly drive past the front of the restaurant. It struck me as strange."

"Do you remember what it looked like?" This might be the break they needed!

She nodded. "Gray, a little bit lighter than this." She gestured toward the rental. "But there's more—I also remember part of the license plate."

Oliver grinned and reached for his phone. "Hop in," he said, already rounding the hood. "I know just who to call."

It didn't take long for Dom to come through.

"Found the car," his brother said as soon as Oliver answered the phone. "Got an address."

"That was fast," Oliver remarked. He gave Hilary a thumbs-up and she nodded, relief plain on her face. She sat on the sofa in the living room area of the hotel suite, her shoulders relaxing for the first time since they'd come back from her parents' home.

"It's not my first rodeo," Dom replied dryly. "So what now? Are you sure you don't want me to give this information to the police?"

"No," Oliver said, shaking his head even though his brother couldn't see him. "We can't involve the cops. The kidnappers were very clear on that." It had taken a bit of convincing before Hilary had agreed to let Oliver call Dom with the information about the car. She'd been terrified of doing anything to antagonize the men who had taken her brother, not wanting him to be hurt.

Or worse.

Personally, Oliver thought the police might be better suited to extracting her brother, especially if they knew where he was being held. But at this point, he didn't want to break Hilary's trust. If the cops acted and Jeff was killed, she'd never forgive him for it.

"That's what I figured," Dom said. "You staying at the Metropolitan?"

"Yes," Oliver replied. "Why?"

"Sit tight," his brother instructed. "I'm on my way to get Ezra and then I'm coming for you."

"You don't need—"

"I'm not letting you go by yourself," Dom interrupted. "So don't even try that."

Oliver smiled to himself, simultaneously irritated and tickled by his brother. "Fine," he said, knowing better than to argue. He could head out on his own, but when Dom and Ezra caught up to him there would be hell to pay.

"I should be there in about half an hour," Dom continued.

"Call me when you're downstairs," Oliver said. "And thanks."

He ended the call and walked over to the sofa to sit down next to Hilary. "Your hunch paid off," he said.

She nodded with a smile. "So I gathered."

"My brothers are on their way here now. We're going to check out the place."

Hilary frowned. "Are you sure that's safe?"

"We'll be fine. Dom is an FBI agent and Ezra was in the army. They know how to handle themselves."

"That's great for them, but what about you?"

Oliver pretended to be offended. "Thanks for the vote of confidence."

She shot him a look. "You know what I mean. As much as I want my brother back, I don't want you to put yourself in danger to make that happen. If something happens to you, we'll really be in trouble!"

Her concern made him feel warm inside, a pleasurable feeling he wished he could take more time to savor. "It's going to be okay," he said seriously. "We're just going to look around, nothing more." *Well, nothing much more*, he amended silently. The truth was he intended to talk to whoever was inside the building, hoping to speed up the exchange process.

Hilary's expression remained doubtful. "Do you promise?"

Oliver met her eyes. "I promise not to take any unnecessary risks." They could argue later about the fluid definition of *unnecessary* once he was back with Jeff.

She pressed her lips together and for a second, he

thought she was going to argue with him. But she settled for a nod.

"All right," she replied. "I suppose that will have to do."

He leaned closer. "I have to say, I like it a little bit when you worry about me." He pushed a strand of hair behind her ear, then let his fingertip trace the curve of her jaw.

"Is that so?" Her voice wobbled a little, making him smile.

"Uh-huh." He nuzzled the side of her neck, causing her to suck in a breath.

"That seems a little twisted." She tilted her head back to give him easier access to the hollow of her throat. The pulse in her neck quickened and he felt his own heart thump hard against his ribs.

"I never said I was normal." He worked his way up her neck, enjoying the raspy sounds of her breathing. Drawing on his self-control, he stopped when he got to her mouth, holding himself back.

Back in the car, he'd been the one to initiate the kiss. And while Hilary had said she wanted him, a small part of him needed her to be the one to make a move now.

Her eyes opened, her gaze a little unfocused. "What's wrong?" she asked.

"Nothing," he replied. "I'm right where I want to be."

Her smile warmed his heart. Then she closed the distance between them and pressed her lips to his.

Her kiss was sweet and tender, a gentle pressure that started out almost hesitant, building to something more as the moment stretched on. The tip of her tongue swiped the underside of his lip, the contact sending zings of sensation through his body.

She reached for him, one hand pressing flat against his chest while the other gripped his shoulder, pulling him closer. He touched her waist, running his hand up the length of her torso to settle his palm along the side of her breast. She was warm and curvy and soft in all the right places, and Oliver wanted nothing more than to lay her out on the bed and spend the next week getting reacquainted with her body.

But he had responsibilities to deal with first. And unless he pumped the brakes, he was going to forget all about his brothers and their impending arrival.

Just the thought of Dom and Ezra pounding on the door to the suite cooled his arousal. Oliver leaned back, breaking the kiss. Hilary made a little sound of protest that tested his resolve, but he knew if he kissed her again, he'd be lost.

"I'm sorry," he said, pressing his forehead to hers. "My brothers will be here in a bit, and I can't afford to get caught up with you yet."

Hilary nodded. "It's okay. I understand."

Oliver leaned back against the sofa, pulling her with him until her head rested against his chest and his arm was around her shoulder. It felt good to hold her like this as a comfortable silence filled the room.

She relaxed against him, some of the tension leaving her body as he idly caressed her back. He knew they still had a lot to discuss, but for now, it was nice to simply be together.

All too soon, the ring of his phone interrupted their peaceful interlude. They both sat up, and as he got to his feet Hilary stood as well. Her frown was back, her lips tight again.

"Be careful." She wrapped her arms around him and squeezed tightly. Oliver returned her embrace, a little surprised as he registered the firm curve of their baby pressed against him. It was a potent reminder that he had a lot to look forward to.

And a lot to lose.

"Try not to worry," he said, kissing her quickly. "I'll be back before you know it."

He released her and walked to the door, a sense of urgency pushing him forward.

The sooner he got this over with, the better.

Chapter 11

Oliver's absence made the hotel suite seem larger and cold somehow, as though all the warmth had left with him.

Hilary found a wrap draped over one of the sitting chairs and draped it around her shoulders. She hated being left behind while Oliver and his brothers went to look at the address Dom had turned up. What exactly was she supposed to do while they were gone? Sit here and look pretty?

After a few minutes of aimless pacing and letting her mind conjure up a few nightmare scenarios, Hilary took a deep breath and forced herself to stop. Oliver had promised he wouldn't take any unnecessary risks, and while she recognized he'd given himself a pretty big loophole, she had to believe his brothers would keep him from doing anything too rash.

She wasn't used to worrying over him. In the past, he'd crossed her mind a time or two…okay, more than that, if she was being honest. But before, she'd always known they didn't have a future together, so she was able to redirect her thoughts. Now, though? With a baby in the picture and the fact they had agreed to try for a real relationship? She'd started to hope. If something happened to him, it would not only crush her; it would change their little family forever.

She had to find a distraction, and fast. Unless she changed course, she'd work herself into a hysteria thinking about all the things that could go wrong, not only for Oliver, but her brother as well.

Spying her phone on a table a few feet away, Hilary walked over and picked it up. There were things she could do until Oliver returned. Her email, for instance. Perhaps her professors had responded to her request for an extension?

They had; all of them told her to take whatever time she needed to heal. Hilary hadn't been that stressed about her schoolwork, but their messages did help relieve her mind a bit. One less thing to worry about.

She rested her free hand on her belly and found herself idly stroking the curve of her baby. Time to find an OB—the emergency room doctor had given her a list of names to try. Where was it?

After a quick search through her bag, she found the page. She returned to the sofa and began to make calls. It didn't take long to find a doctor who was accepting both new patients and her insurance plan. The first available appointment was next Monday. Hopefully Oliver would be able to go with her...

She ended the call and stared at her phone. Where was Oliver now? How long would it take for them to scope out the place and get back?

Hilary walked to her bedroom and finished unpacking, hanging her clothes in the closet and placing items in the large dresser. Then she wandered aimlessly through the rooms of the suite, running her hand along the fabric of chairs, stopping to take in the view from different windows. It was a beautiful space, and if the circumstances were different, she would have loved all the little touches of luxury.

But they were lost on her at the moment.

She found herself in the bedroom Oliver had slept in last night. The housekeeping staff had come through while they were at her parents' house, so the room was impeccable. Even so, she could tell he had occupied this space. There was something in the air, an intangible quality that reminded her of him.

She walked over to the bed and pulled down the covers, then slipped under them. Pressing her nose to one of the pillows, she drew in a deep breath and was rewarded with a hint of Oliver's scent. She closed her eyes and hugged the pillow close, imagining he was there with her. It was a poor substitute for his actual presence, but it would have to do for now.

Hilary felt herself relax, her body sinking into the soft comfort of the bed. She imagined Oliver there with her and drifted off to sleep with a smile.

After a quick stop at the bank, Oliver settled into the back seat of Dom's truck.

"So what's your plan?"

"My plan?" Oliver repeated.

Dom eyed him in the rearview mirror. "Yes. What do you intend to do once we get to this place?"

Oliver shrugged. "I'm going to talk to the guy and offer him money." He'd thought that was obvious, given their small detour.

Dom and Ezra exchanged a glance in the front of the truck. "You might want to rethink that strategy," Ezra advised.

"I don't think it's going to work out the way you want," Dom agreed.

Oliver refrained from rolling his eyes. "I know it's not ideal, but it's the only way to get Jeff released quickly."

"Wouldn't you rather take some time to figure out a better plan?" Dom asked. "Once you pay, they'll keep bleeding you for money."

"We have to get Hilary's brother back first," Oliver said. "Once he's safe, we can strategize all you want."

His brothers exchanged another look. "Roger that," Ezra said.

It was time to change the subject. Oliver appreciated his brothers going with him, but he didn't want to spend the drive being lectured. "How are Theresa and the girls?"

"All good," Ezra replied. His voice softened at the mention of his new family he was building with Theresa Fitzgerald and her daughters. "I've been able to get some work done on the house since I've been on leave."

"Weren't you supposed to be resting and recovering?" Dom asked. Ezra had been shot a few months ago, and during the operation to treat him, the doctors had removed his spleen. He'd been under strict instructions to take it easy, but apparently Ezra had considered the doctor's orders to be more like suggestions.

"I'm fine," Ezra grumbled with a dismissive wave of his hand.

"When do you return to active duty?" Oliver asked.

"Well, that's the thing," Ezra said. "I don't think I'm going to."

"What?" Dom and Oliver spoke together, both apparently equally shocked by their brother's statement.

Ezra shrugged. "I've done enough time to retire. It would make Theresa feel a lot better if I stayed close to home instead of going off on deployment for months at a time. She and the girls have already lost so much. If something happened to me, I don't know how they'd cope."

"Wow." Oliver had never expected to hear his brother talk like this. Ezra's career in the army did put him in danger, but that had never seemed to bother him before. It was the same for Dom— he'd loved working undercover. It seemed love had changed both of his brothers and recalibrated their tolerance for risk.

It was having the same effect on him as well. Sure, his job wasn't dangerous, but now that he and Hilary were trying to build a relationship and they had a baby on the way, he was going to have to make major adjustments to his travel schedule.

"What are you going to do?" Dom asked. "I'm sure Theresa will be glad to have you close, but I doubt she'll be happy with you being jobless."

"I've been thinking about starting my own security company," Ezra replied. "I've got some expertise in that area, and I have friends from the service who are willing to sign on."

"Do you need an investor?" Oliver said. "Because I'd be happy to back you. In fact, I might sign up as your first client. I could probably use a bodyguard if this thing drags on too long."

Ezra chuckled. "I'm always happy to take your money, brother."

"What about a partner?" Dom asked quietly.

Oliver and Ezra both turned to look at him. "Are you looking to make a change, too?" Ezra said.

"Maybe," Dom replied. "The desk job just isn't doing it for me and I'm tired of the commute. Plus, I don't want Sami to have to move her business. She's well established here, so it makes sense for me to find something else rather than ask her to uproot everything and start over in Denver with me."

"I'd love to have you join me," Ezra replied. "Have you guys set a date for the wedding yet?"

"Soon," Dom said. "We're still looking at venues. Once we make a decision on that front, a lot will depend on availability."

"Makes sense," Oliver said. He'd never considered that aspect of picking a wedding date before, but then again, he'd never been responsible for planning a celebration like that, either.

"What about you?" Ezra asked, glancing into the back seat. "The fact that you're involved in trying to get Hilary's brother released suggests there's something going on there."

Oliver considered denying it, but what would be the point? His triplet brothers knew him better than anyone else; he wouldn't disrespect them by trying to downplay his feelings for Hilary. Besides, his earlier conversation and decision with Hilary to try to have a real relationship had left him feeling a combination of happy, excited and eager. For the first time in a long time, he was looking forward to the future of his personal life, rather than focusing solely on his professional goals.

"Funny you should ask," he started. "Yes, Hilary and I are together."

Dom reached over to smack Ezra's leg. "Told you. Pay up."

Oliver rolled his eyes. "There's a bit more to it," he said.

"When's she due?" Dom asked.

Oliver felt his jaw drop. "Seriously? How did you possibly guess that?"

Dom threw his head back and laughed. "Just lucky. I had no idea. But when you said there was more to it, I made an assumption."

"You know what they say about assuming," Ezra said dryly.

"Yeah, but in this case I'm not the ass," Dom shot back.

"Sure you are," Oliver replied. "Way to steal my thunder."

"Sorry," Dom said, sounding only a little contrite. "I can't believe you're actually going to be a father!"

Oliver nodded, though his brothers weren't looking at him. "Same. She just found out. It was a shock to both of us."

Ezra angled in his seat to glance back at Oliver. "I take it you went back to the restaurant after I beat you at pool that night?"

Oliver merely smiled.

"That was a few months ago," Dom said, clearly doing the math. "So that means the baby will be here in… February?"

"April," corrected Ezra. "Babies take forty weeks to cook. That works out to ten months."

Oliver was surprised by his brother's knowledge of pregnancy, but given the fact that Theresa had twins of her own, they'd probably talked about babies before.

Dom whistled. "That'll be here before you know it," he said. "Does this mean you're going to settle down in Blue Larkspur? Or are you still going to travel the world?"

"There's a lot I can do from here," Oliver said. "There might be a few trips that I have to make, but I think I'll be able to do most of my work remotely. I definitely intend on being here for the baby, so it will be an adjustment. But Hilary and I are going to try to have a real relationship, and I'm going to make it work. I'm not going to make the same kind of mistakes Dad did. I plan on being there for my kid."

"I hear that," Dom said. "I think the one good thing to come out of the mess with dad is that we all want to make better choices."

"Mom will be thrilled," Ezra remarked. "Having all three of us around again? She'll love it."

"Yeah, but maybe we should tell her about all of this in stages," Dom joked. "You starting a business, me moving here and Oliver having a baby? It's a lot to take in all at once."

"Fair enough," Ezra said.

They joked and chatted as Dom steered them through Blue Larkspur, heading north. The scenery changed from neighborhoods and small businesses to more industrial-type buildings and bail bondsmen, eventually thinning out into warehouses and used car lots.

Dom glanced over at Ezra. "Are you armed?"

Alarm spiked through Oliver. Did his brother think they would need guns? He'd just planned on talking to the guy, not shooting anyone.

Ezra shook his head. "You?"

"No." Dom turned off onto a gravel drive and slowed as the truck began to hit pothole after pothole. "Trying not to escalate things."

"Sounds good," Ezra said. "Let's hope they agree." He nodded toward the warehouse they were approaching, indicating the large man leaning against the frame of the open bay door. He was tall, muscular, and dressed in black jeans and a black shirt. Dom parked the truck and spoke to Oliver, though his eyes never left the guy.

"Sure you want to do this?"

Oliver swallowed. He was used to doing business in boardrooms while wearing a suit. This was somewhat outside the realm of both his experience and comfort zone. But it had to be done. "Yes."

The three of them climbed out of the truck and moved to stand in front of it. The guard straightened and walked over, taking a last drag off his cigarette before tossing it to the ground.

"This is private property."

"We're here to see Vince Doherty."

Two other men stepped out of the open bay and started over, moving to flank them. From the corner of his eye, he saw Dom and Ezra shift slightly and he recognized the tension in their bodies. The three of them had gotten into their share of scuffles over the years, mostly with each other. Unless he missed his guess, his brothers were preparing to fight if necessary.

The man angled his head to the side. "Mr. Doherty doesn't want to be seen."

Oliver hadn't come out here to be brushed aside so easily. "It's about Jeff Weston." He glanced at the man to his left. "Tell him I'll make it worth his time."

The goon glanced at the man in the middle, who was clearly in charge. The head honcho nodded, and the guy disappeared through the open bay. Oliver relaxed slightly; two on three was slightly better odds, even though he wasn't much of a fighter anymore.

The man returned and spoke quietly to the guy in charge. The smoker stared at Oliver while he listened, then nodded. "All right," he said. "You can come in."

Oliver and his brothers took a step forward, only to stop when the man held up a hand. "Whoa. Just you. Your friends stay here."

Dom's jaw tightened, but he said nothing. Ezra looked at Oliver. "Are you on board with this?"

Oliver nodded. "I'll be fine. We're just going to talk, remember?"

He stepped forward and was subjected to a quick

frisking before being led inside the dark interior of the warehouse. The place was lined with metal shelves that were stacked high with boxes. It smelled of oil and gasoline, though he didn't see any engines around. There was an office at the far end, light glowing through the cracks in the wooden blinds that were drawn over the windows. There was no sign of Jeff, but Oliver hadn't expected him to be out in the middle of everything.

The man knocked on the closed door. A muffled voice told them to come in, and he pushed open the door and ushered Oliver inside.

Oliver took a few steps, stopping in front of a large wooden desk in the center of the room. A set of filing cabinets flanked the desk, and the walls were full of framed photos of classic cars.

A rather ordinary-looking man sat behind the desk. Thanks to a few too many gangster movies, Oliver had expected to see a guy with slicked-back dark hair wearing a shiny suit. Instead, this man had light brown hair combed to the side, and he wore a polo shirt tucked into khaki pants. He looked like a middle school teacher or perhaps an accountant, not a loan shark.

"I understand you want to talk to me about Jeff Weston." It wasn't a question—he spoke with the certainty of a man in charge.

Oliver nodded. "Yes, that's right. You're Vince Doherty?"

"Who are you?" Vince tilted his head to the side,

assessing Oliver with the kind of curiosity a child might display when examining a strange bug.

"Oliver Colton," he replied. Best not to overshare; he'd answer Doherty's questions but offer nothing else. He didn't trust this man and didn't want to give any information he could use against him.

"How do you know Jeff?"

"I don't." Oliver shrugged, trying to act casual. "But a friend of mine does. His absence is very distressing to some people I care about. I was hoping we might come to an arrangement."

Vince steepled his fingers under his nose. "And you thought I was the person to contact?"

Oliver nodded. "I have friends who hear things. They all said you'd have answers for me."

"I see." Vince studied him a moment, apparently assessing his sincerity. "Let's assume I can help you. What kind of arrangement did you have in mind?"

"I'm willing to pay Jeff's debt. I'll give you ten thousand right now, provided you release him."

Vince made a show of looking around the room. "Release him? I certainly don't have him."

Oliver played along. "I believe you know where he is?"

"Maybe I do. But he owes more than ten thousand. What about the rest?"

"I'll pay the balance a week from today."

"What are you offering as collateral?"

"My word?"

Vince's lips twitched with a smile. "Try again."

Oliver sighed and tried to come up with something he could offer to show Doherty he was good for the money. He crossed his arms, his watch sliding up his wrist. In a flash of inspiration, Oliver unfastened the Rolex and passed it to Vince.

Vince took the watch and studied it carefully. "This is either genuine, or it's the best fake I've ever seen." He handed it back to Oliver.

"It's the real deal," Oliver told him. He'd splurged on the watch to celebrate after his first big deal had gone through, figuring it would be the last watch he'd ever need to buy. He'd worn it for the better part of a decade, a subtle statement piece that was an important part of his professional image as a successful venture capitalist. "This is real, too." He reached into his back pocket and withdrew an envelope of cash, placing it on Vince's desk.

Doherty picked up the envelope and thumbed through the bills inside. He set the envelope back on his desk and nodded.

"All right, Mr. Colton. We have a deal. I'll see to it that your friend finds his way home again."

Oliver breathed a sigh of relief. "Thank you." He moved to go, but Vince held up his hand.

"Not so fast. I expect you back here with the balance of my money in one week's time. If you fail to show up by noon, Tony is going to come looking for you." He nodded in the direction of the hulking man who had accompanied Oliver through the warehouse. "Tony is not as…patient as I am when it comes to dealing with people. Do you understand my meaning?"

Oliver nodded. "I do. It won't be an issue."

"I hope not. For your sake," Vince added. "Because should Tony be unable to find you, he'll be forced to talk to someone you care about. And let me tell you, the harder Tony has to search for answers, the grumpier he gets."

Hilary's face flashed in Oliver's mind. The thought of this man getting anywhere near her was enough to make his blood run cold.

"As I told you," Oliver replied evenly. "You'll get the rest of your money next week. I have no intention of defaulting."

Vince's eyes were cold. "No one ever does."

"Thanks for your time," Oliver said, deciding to change the subject. He didn't want to give Doherty the impression that he was afraid of him. Growing up with brothers had taught Oliver that showing fear was the fastest way to become a target. "I'll see you next week."

"Looking forward to it," Vince replied. He gestured to Tony, who took a step forward. "Tony will see you to your truck. Tell your brothers hello."

How did he—? *Cameras*, Oliver decided. He must have a feed from security cameras streaming on his computer screen. He'd watched them arrive, possibly even run Dom's plates and learned his address. A chill ran down Oliver's spine as he realized he'd underestimated Doherty. He wasn't just some small-time loan shark—he was a smart man who made a living in the seedier underbelly of Blue Larkspur. And while Oliver wasn't afraid for himself, he worried that he'd just put his brothers in the crosshairs of a predator. Even though he planned to settle with Vince, the criminal might not be willing to let him go so easily. Especially once he learned the extent of Oliver's assets.

But there was no time for regrets now. He'd made a deal with the devil, and he couldn't back out. Jeff, and more importantly Hilary, were counting on him.

Chapter 12

Hilary stretched, arching her spine as she slowly opened her eyes. The bed was warm, and her body felt loose and completely relaxed for the first time in…well, since she'd slept with Oliver.

The mattress shifted slightly behind her, and she realized she was no longer alone. An arm slipped around her waist, drawing her back against a solid wall of man.

"How was your nap?" Oliver's voice was a low rumble in her ear, the sound reverberating through her body in a delicious tingle.

Hilary sighed. "Wonderful. I didn't actually mean to sleep, but I lay down and the next thing I know you're here." Then the implications of his presence hit her and she pushed herself upright. "You're here!"

Oliver rolled onto his back, propping his head on his folded arms. He grinned up at her, looking so tempting that her concentration began to falter. "In the flesh."

Forcing her thoughts back on track, Hilary resisted the temptation to touch him. "What happened? What did the place look like?"

"It was a warehouse on the edge of town. I spoke with Doherty, and he's agreed to release your brother."

Shock rolled over her in a wave. "Are you serious?" She was reduced to sputtering. "When?"

"Soon," Oliver replied. "I wouldn't be surprised if Jeff turns up within the hour."

Happiness and relief flooded her system. She threw herself against Oliver, hugging him as best as she could given their positions. "I can't believe it! What did he say?" Then she remembered the original purpose of their trip. "Wait." She pulled back, frowning down at him. "You said you were just going to look at the place, not go inside or talk to anyone."

A guilty look flashed across Oliver's face. "I didn't have much choice," he said, sounding sheepish. "There was a guy standing outside who watched us drive up."

Hilary raised one eyebrow, not buying it. "Uh-huh. Did he force you out of the car?"

"Not exactly. But it would have been rude to ignore him."

Hilary lightly smacked his chest with the back of her hand. "You said you were going to be careful!" This man and his goons had assaulted her and kidnapped her brother. The thought of Oliver meeting with him made her blood run cold. What if he'd said something to offend the guy? What if Doherty simply hadn't liked the look of Oliver's face? He might have taken Oliver, too, or hurt him in some way.

The intensity of her reaction gave her pause. She'd spent the past months burying her emotions where Oliver was concerned. Apparently, all the recent developments between them had blown the lid off that mental box and now she was at the mercy of her feelings.

"I was careful," Oliver said. "I was on my best behavior, and my brothers were waiting for me outside."

Hilary sucked in a breath. "They didn't go inside with you?" That was even worse. This whole time, she'd thought his brothers would help keep the situation under control. But it seemed they had missed the most dangerous part of the whole trip!

Oliver seemed to realize his mistake. His eyes widened. "Ah, the office was pretty small. There wasn't enough room for all of us."

Hilary shifted, putting some distance between them. It seemed Oliver had taken full advantage of the loophole in his earlier promise. And while everything had worked out for the best, Hilary felt a little betrayed by his actions.

Apparently sensing her distress, Oliver sat up and reached for her. "Hey, it's okay. I needed to talk to the guy, and that's what I did. I made my offer and he accepted it. Your brother is coming home and I'm here now, still in one piece. There's nothing for you to worry about anymore."

She let herself be drawn back against his chest. He tucked her head under his neck and stroked one hand down her back, his touch soothing.

He was right; she recognized her concern wasn't necessary now that the event was over. Still, it bothered her to know that while Oliver had been putting himself at risk for the sake of her family, she'd been sleeping in his bed.

What would you have done? asked a mocking voice in her head. Awake or asleep, she wouldn't have been able to accomplish anything from the hotel suite. But…he could have called her. He could have sent her a message to keep her up to speed. She'd assumed they were merely going to look around. Oliver should have told her about the change in plans.

"I wish you had let me know."

"Why does it matter now?" He sounded genuinely puzzled, as though he couldn't understand why she was making a big deal out of his meeting with the loan shark.

Hilary took a deep breath, trying to organize her thoughts so she could explain them in a way that made sense. "I know you're used to doing things on your own, but we're a team now—at least when it comes to this. And your choices don't just affect you anymore. I don't want to stifle you, but when you do something risky like that, you're not the only one who could end up hurt."

He cupped the side of her face with his hand and gazed deeply into her eyes. "Okay," he said simply.

"Okay?" she repeated, wondering if this was a trick. Did he really understand her perspective, or was he simply trying to appease her so they could move on?

"I hadn't thought of it that way, but you're right," he continued. "I'm sorry I went beyond what I said I was going to do. I saw an opportunity and I took it, but I didn't think about how it might affect you."

"Thank you," she said. She glanced away, feeling a little silly now. "Don't get me wrong—I'm grateful for what you did and I'm happy it was a successful trip. It's just the thought of something happening to you and my brother..." She trailed off, shuddering as a dark cloud passed over her thoughts.

Oliver's hand was warm on her skin. "Nothing happened," he assured her quietly. "I'm here. Jeff is coming home. You don't have to worry anymore."

She wanted to believe him, and in this moment, it was easy to think that everything would work out for the best. He was here with her, Jeff was on the verge of being released and her parents didn't have to sell the restaurant. What more could she ask for?

He guided her down to the mattress again, putting her head on his chest and laying his arm around her. She heard his heart beating steadily under her ear, a comforting thump that gave her something to focus on so she could redirect her worried thoughts.

Months ago, she would have never believed she'd be here with Oliver. In her wildest dreams, she'd entertained the fantasy of something long-term with him, but in her heart she'd known it wasn't going to happen.

Except now it was.

"What are you thinking about?" he asked softly.

"You," she replied simply.

"Should I be flattered?" His hand ran lazily along her side, but there was nothing demanding about his touch.

Hilary smiled, though he couldn't see her face. "I never thought I'd be with you again, not like this. I mean, I'd hoped, but I knew it wasn't going to happen because our lives are so different."

He was quiet for a few seconds. "I thought about you every day. I know that's hard to believe because I didn't call you, but you were definitely on my mind."

"Really?" His confession made her feel warm inside. It was nice to know he'd missed her, since he'd been a permanent fixture in her brain.

"Yeah," he confirmed. "That night with you made me realize I wanted to make some changes. That's why I stopped by the restaurant once I got to town. If you hadn't shut me down, I'd like to think we would have found our way to each other again."

Hilary considered his words for a moment. "Maybe so. I didn't realize you were looking to settle down. I thought you just wanted a repeat of our night together."

He stopped stroking her arm. "You're more than just a warm body to me. I'm sorry that I didn't make that clear."

She rested her hand on his chest. "I should have been more willing to listen."

He chuckled softly. "I don't blame you. It's not like I had stayed in touch. I can't fault you for assuming the worst when I showed up again."

"I guess in some ways I should be happy Jeff got himself into trouble," she said wryly. "If he hadn't, we would have gone our separate ways again."

"This is much better," Oliver said. "I'm glad I get to be here with you for most of the pregnancy."

"Me, too." Even though she and Oliver were still getting to know each other, it was good to have him by her side as she learned more about the baby. She told him about her upcoming doctor's appointment.

"Can I come with you?"

"I was hoping you would." It was nice of him to ask, though, rather than simply assume that she'd want him there.

"Do you think we'll get to hear the heartbeat?" There was a note of excitement in his voice that made her smile. "There's a heart by now, right?"

"I think so," Hilary replied. "I haven't had a chance to do much reading on fetal development, but I think the heart forms pretty early on."

"Amazing," he said softly. She couldn't help but agree.

Hilary shifted, angling her body to put some space between them. Then she took Oliver's free hand and placed it over her bump.

He went still, as though his whole consciousness was attuned to the mystery inside her. "Can you feel anything yet?" His voice was barely above a whisper.

"No," she admitted. "I hope soon, though." She looked up and smiled at him. "You don't have to whisper, though. You're not going to bother her. Or him."

He blinked, then laughed. "I didn't even realize I'd done that. But you're right."

He was so handsome in that moment, his blue eyes sparkling with joy, his face relaxed and his smile genuine. Unable to resist the temptation, Hilary reached for him and pulled his head down for a kiss.

It started out easy, a simple connection. A way to feel closer to him. But as soon as she felt his lips against hers, her body began to warm. Within a few seconds she felt like a furnace was roaring inside of her, spreading heat throughout her limbs.

Oliver dipped his tongue inside her mouth to brush along hers. The contact sent zings of sensation to her core, stoking her growing need.

She moaned softly, gripping his shoulders as she

strained to get closer to him. She wanted to feel the length of him against her, press her curves to his solid strength. The last few months had been stressful and lonely. Oliver's big body offered a promise of comfort and safety, a refuge from her worries.

If only for a little bit.

His hand moved from her belly, roaming north until he found one of her breasts. She sighed as he cupped her—he'd been the last man to touch her there. It was only fitting he be the one to do so now.

Oliver moved, rolling her until she was flat on her back. He leaned over her, settling his weight on top of her. Then he froze and pulled away.

"What? What's wrong?" Hilary struggled to adjust to his sudden change. Had something happened? What was going on?

He lay next to her, looking guilty. "I don't want to crush you or the baby," he explained.

Hilary couldn't help but laugh. "You won't," she said. "I'm sure it's fine."

He frowned slightly, traces of doubt still on his face. "Are you certain?"

Hilary pulled him over her again, smiling at the careful way he settled his weight. She could tell by the tension in his body that he wasn't totally relaxed, but hopefully she could show him that he didn't have to treat her like glass.

She reached for him, intending to bring him closer for another kiss. But he hesitated again.

"I'm really okay," she said, trying to reassure him that he wasn't hurting her.

"No, that's not it." He searched her face, clearly looking for a sign of some kind. "It's just, are you sure you want to do this?"

She stiffened. "Are you not interested?"

He scoffed. "I certainly am." He moved slightly until she felt his hard length along her thigh. "But I don't want you to feel pressured or think that you owe me for the thing with your brother."

Hilary relaxed back against the mattress, relieved to know he wasn't rejecting her. "Trust me, Jeff is the last thing on my mind right now. I want you for you."

It was the truth. Now that they had talked about their relationship, Hilary wanted to take the next step. She needed to be with Oliver again, have that physical reassurance of their connection to each other.

Oliver's doubt seemed to fade away, leaving him watching her with a hunger in his eyes that made her stomach do a little flip. "Good," he breathed, leaning down. "Because I don't want to stop."

God, he'd missed her.

Oliver pressed his mouth to Hilary's, reveling in the taste of her. How had he gone months without this? Without holding her in his arms, feeling her against his body? Breathing her in, sensing her warmth.

At least he never had to miss her again.

He didn't know how he was going to make the transition to working from Blue Larkspur. But he was going to do whatever it took, as long as it meant coming home to Hilary every night.

She shifted under him, her curves pressing against him. The contact heightened his arousal, sending his blood racing. It roared in his ears as he slowly worked his way down her neck, tracing the line of her throat with the tip of his tongue.

She shivered, letting out a soft moan that went straight to his groin. He pushed the hem of her shirt up, increasing his access to her skin. He cupped her breasts, the satin of her bra doing little to hide her nipples.

Hilary gasped as he took one in his mouth and sucked gently. She rolled her hips, seeking more contact. Oliver was only too happy to oblige.

His hands caressed her torso as he worked her shirt over her head, then tossed it to the floor. Her bra was next, and then he focused on her pants, drawing the rest of her clothes slowly down her legs.

Then she was naked, her beautiful body exposed to his gaze. His breath caught in his throat as he looked at her, curvy and soft in all the right places. He'd never wanted a woman more, and part of him marveled at the fact that she wanted to be with him after everything he'd put her through.

Hilary didn't try to cover herself. She let him look his fill, content to be the focus of his attention. When he finally met her eyes, she smiled faintly. "The least you could do is return the favor."

He didn't need to be asked twice. Oliver stripped off his clothes in record time, throwing them carelessly to the floor. He leaned over to cover her again, but she held up her hand, stalling him.

"It's my turn to look."

She sat up, gently shoving him until he was on his back, stretched out on the mattress. Hilary ran her eyes over him, her gaze so hot he could practically feel it as it moved down the length of his body and back again.

"Very nice," she murmured, leaning over to touch, to caress, to kiss. Her words were like a shot in the arm to his ego, which inflated along with his need for her.

She wrapped her hand around his length, making soft sounds of approval as she began to stroke him. Oliver gasped and nearly came off the bed as she touched him, working him with a rhythm that made him see stars. Then she took him in her mouth and his brain short-circuited.

Shaking with need, he eased her off him. "Not yet," he said, his voice ragged.

Hilary's smile was pure feminine satisfaction. She was far too composed, too in control. He couldn't let that stand.

Moving quickly, Oliver rolled her onto her back and hitched her knees over his shoulders. Before she knew what was going on, he fastened his mouth on her and began his own torture.

Hilary writhed against him, her hands threading through his hair as he pleasured her. She filled his senses, his world shrinking to her and her alone. Her moans were music to his ears, urging him on. She cried out his name, her body going stiff under him. Then she shuddered and relaxed, going boneless on the bed.

Oliver worked his way up her stomach, easing her down from her release. Hilary opened her eyes as he reached her face.

"That wasn't fair," she said.

He grinned down at her. "I never said I played fair."

She hooked her legs around his waist pulled him forward. He jumped as she touched him, bringing him to the entrance of her body. "Neither do I," she said, lifting her hips as she drew him into her.

Oliver couldn't hold back a groan as her warmth surrounded him. Instinct took over and he began to move, rocking into her in time with his heartbeat.

Emotions filled him, building in his chest until it felt like his body was too small to contain them all. She was his, body and soul. And he belonged to her.

Completely.

She reached up and touched the side of his face, her touch so tender it almost broke him. His release began to build, crowding out everything else.

"Hilary." He gasped out her name, wanting to say this before he couldn't. "I love you."

She smiled up at him, her body gripping his tightly. "I love you, too."

The sound of her voice and the warmth of her embrace pushed him over the edge. His completion rushed through him on a wave of intense pleasure, leaving him breathless. He sank onto the mattress, angling to the side so as not to crush her with his deadweight.

Hilary stroked his back gently as his brain started working again. "Did you mean it?" she asked softly.

He didn't need to ask what she was talking about. "Yes," he said, rolling onto his side so he could look at her. "I did."

He'd never said those words to anyone before. Well, not anyone who wasn't family. But it wasn't just the sex talking. Hilary was the one for him—he knew it. A sense of rightness washed over him, confirming he'd done the right thing by telling her.

A series of emotions flickered across her face. She opened her mouth, then closed it. After a few seconds she spoke. "I've never had a man say that to me before," she confessed.

Oliver reached out to brush her hair off her cheek, tucking the strands behind her ear. "We have something in common," he said with a smile. "I've never said that to a woman before."

She blinked at him. "Really?"

"You sound surprised."

"I am," she said. "I mean, your life always looked so glamorous to me. You were always on the go, and it seemed like you always had a beautiful woman on your arm."

"I've had my share of relationships," he allowed, "but none of them were serious. The women I dated weren't looking for anything long-term. We had our fun and parted ways. Until I got involved with you, I figured that was what my life would be like."

Hilary glanced away. "And now you're going to be a father. Which is about as permanent as it gets."

"That's true." He caressed the side of her face until she looked at him again. "But I wouldn't have it any other way."

"If…" She trailed off, then tried again. "If it wasn't for the baby…"

She didn't need to finish. "I told you earlier," he said softly. "It's always been you. The baby is the icing on the cake."

Hilary nodded slightly. "I'm sorry," she said. "I just needed to hear you say it again. My mind keeps circling around what would have happened between us if I wasn't pregnant. I can't shake the sense that we wouldn't be here, together, if it wasn't for the baby."

"I know what you mean." He'd had similar thoughts, but they didn't plague him in the same way. "I'd like to think we still would have come together eventually."

"Yeah," she said softly.

He kissed the tip of her nose. "The important

thing is that we're here now. The pregnancy is a shortcut, helping us skip to the end without having to spend more time apart before we figured this out."

She laughed, a spark coming back into her eyes. "That's a nice way of putting it."

He pulled her closer, wanting to feel her against him again. She was warm and soft and so perfect.

Hilary sighed, throwing her leg over his hip as she snuggled against him. Oliver's arousal began to build again, but before he could do anything about it, her phone rang.

She stiffened and looked up at him. "I'm sorry," she said, already pulling away. "Normally I wouldn't, but with everything going on—"

"Don't worry about it," he assured her. "I understand." Hopefully it was news that Jeff had been released and was home safely.

He got a nice view of her bottom as she rolled over and reached for her phone. Distracted by thoughts of what he wanted to do to her, he was only dimly aware of her voice as she took the call. After a moment, she said goodbye, then twisted around to face him.

He could tell by her expression the news was good. Hilary's eyes were bright, her skin flushed and her lips curved up in a smile of genuine happiness. Oliver's heart skipped a beat at the sight, and a swell of pride rose in his chest, knowing he'd been the one to put that look on her face.

"That was my dad," she said. "Jeff just walked through the door!"

Chapter 13

After the call, Hilary and Oliver retired to their separate bathrooms to shower. A big part of her wasn't ready to let him go yet, but she wanted to see her brother and she knew it would mean a lot to her parents to have them all together after this ordeal.

"Maybe we could shower together?" she'd suggested.

Oliver had laughed. "I don't think so. If we do that, we won't see your family until tomorrow."

He'd kissed her then, lingering until her blood ran hot. Then he'd pulled away with a groan, leaving her wanting more.

She'd showered and dressed quickly, her mind on Oliver and the moment they'd just shared.

He loved her.

Hearing him say those words had filled her with such happiness. And to know she was the only woman he'd ever confessed to loving made the experience even more special.

It was hard to believe how quickly things had turned around. She'd gone from lying injured in a hospital bed, shocked to learn she was pregnant to getting dressed in a luxury hotel suite, her skin still tingling from the memories of Oliver's touch.

Jeff was back, safe at home. And her parents no longer had to sell Atria. She and Oliver were in a good place emotionally, and she had high hopes for their future together and the family they were building. It was enough to make her cheeks ache from smiling so much.

She glanced out the window as she sat in the passenger seat of Oliver's rental car as he drove them to Atria.

"I can't believe they released him already."

Oliver glanced at her as he navigated a turn. "Why is that?"

She shrugged. "I mean, he had the money. What was to stop him from keeping Jeff longer, or even killing him?"

A smile ghosted across Oliver's face. "You're vicious, aren't you?"

Hilary laughed. "Maybe. But seriously, though, I guess I didn't trust this guy would hold up his end of the bargain."

"Maybe he knew if he didn't, I'd go to the cops?" Oliver suggested. "Men like that don't want to deal with the police if they can avoid it. I'm sure he knew if he didn't follow through, I'd come back, this time with more official support."

Once again, she was glad Oliver and his brothers had left the encounter with the loan shark unharmed.

Her stomach felt like it was full of butterflies as they pulled into the parking lot of Atria. She hadn't been here since the attack, but that wasn't what bothered her now. She was excited to see Jeff, but also still deeply angry with him for racking up so much gambling debt and keeping it a secret from her.

Oliver turned off the engine and gave her hand a squeeze. "Ready?"

She nodded. "Let's go check on him."

The door to the restaurant was locked. A sign was taped to the surface, explaining the place was closed for a private event. Hilary took her keys from her bag and opened things up, then she and Oliver stepped inside. She heard the lock click behind her and gave him a smile of thanks over her shoulder.

The scent of garlic and oregano hung in the air, growing stronger as they walked through the dining area toward the kitchen.

"Hello?" Hilary called out. She heard the din of voices behind the swinging door and realized her family was clustered in the back. Anticipation bubbled in her stomach as they drew closer.

Her father poked his head into the dining area.

"Hilary! Oliver! We're all in here. Come join us." He grinned at her as she and Oliver drew closer, and she saw in a glance that all the tension and stress of the last couple of days had vanished from his face.

He grabbed her in a tight hug, releasing her only to embrace Oliver. "Thank you so much," he said quietly. "You brought him back to us."

Hilary pushed through the swinging door and found her mother standing next to her brother, both of them at one of the prep counters. Cheryl had her hand on her son's shoulder and unless she missed her guess, Hilary didn't think her mom would ever let Jeff out of her sight again.

Her mother turned and saw her, her face lighting up with joy. "Hilary! He's home— isn't it wonderful?" The older woman's eyes filled with tears that she rapidly blinked away.

Hilary studied her mom as she approached. She looked much better than when Hilary had seen her last, but this experience had aged her. The lines on her face were deeper somehow, and the dark circles under her eyes were more pronounced. If Jeff did something like this again, her mother might not survive.

Still, seeing the older woman happy again caused a weight to lift off Hilary's shoulders. There would be time to talk to Jeff privately later. For now, Hilary planned to enjoy this time with her family, and celebrate Oliver's growing role in her life.

Hilary hugged her mom, then turned her attention

to her brother. He stood chopping an onion, but his knife skills were sharp enough to allow him to glance at her in greeting. She sucked in a breath at the sight of his face—he sported a black eye, a busted lip, and there was a deep, angry-looking scrape along his cheekbone. He'd clearly been through the wringer, but at least he'd survived.

Jeff scooped the onions into a pan, then wiped his hands on a towel and turned toward her. He studied her face for a second, then opened his arms. Hilary stepped close, hugging him.

Before she knew what was happening, all the tension and worry from the last couple of days bubbled to the surface and she found herself crying against her brother's chest.

"I'm so sorry," he said softly. "When I saw you on the ground, I didn't know what to do. The guys had to knock me out to get me to stop. I'll never forgive myself for what happened to you."

"Why didn't you tell me?" she asked. "You've been such a bear lately. Why didn't you just let me know what was going on? I could have helped you!"

"Absolutely not," Jeff said firmly. "This was my problem. I wasn't going to drag you into it. You've got your own stuff going on, working on your degree. I wasn't about to burden you with my issues."

Hilary sniffed, exasperated by his words. "You're an idiot."

"I know," Jeff replied. He squeezed her gently,

then leaned back to look at her. "But I'm working on it."

She smiled faintly and stepped away, then noticed Oliver standing a few feet away. He was watching them, a look of satisfaction on his face.

Jeff followed her gaze and noticed Oliver. "Excuse me," he said quietly, walking over to Oliver. The two of them moved a few feet away to talk. Hilary wanted desperately to hear what her brother was saying, but she knew she needed to give them privacy.

Her mother distracted her, walking over and slipping her arm around Hilary's waist. "He won't talk about what happened," she said, looking at the two men with watery eyes. "They beat him up, but he refuses to go to the hospital."

Hilary heard the worry in her mother's voice and turned to face her. "He'll be okay," she said, trying to sound confident. "His face looks bad now, but it will heal. So will the rest of his bruises." But hopefully the lesson from this experience would remain fresh for years to come.

Her father joined them, draping his arm around her shoulder so she was framed between her parents. "I'm so glad you're here," he said. "I can't tell you how much it means to your mother and me to have us all together again."

A sense of peace settled over her as she turned to face her dad. He and her mom weren't the only ones who were happy to have this ordeal behind them.

Being here with her family and with Oliver made her hopeful for the future.

Now she could start planning for it.

Oliver listened with half an ear as Jeff thanked him profusely for paying off part of his debt. It wasn't that he didn't appreciate the gratitude; he did, and he was glad that Jeff appeared to take the situation seriously. But right now, he'd rather be with Hilary.

"I'm going to pay you back. I mean it," Jeff said.

Oliver focused fully on him. "Don't worry about it now," he said. "We have time to figure out the details of that later. I think what's most important is that you get treatment for your gambling addiction."

Jeff's face fell. "Yeah," he said quietly. "I thought I had it under control, but I see now that I didn't. I guess I should do something about it."

Oliver clapped him on the shoulder. "You have a lot of support from your family. You owe it to yourself and to them to take back your life."

Jeff nodded. "You're right. I know you are. I just feel like it's going to be really hard."

"Oh, it will be," Oliver replied. "But speaking from experience, people can change if they want to. Don't let this one issue define your life."

A glint of determination entered Jeff's eyes. "Okay," he said slowly. "I won't."

Oliver nodded and took a step, intending to return to Hilary. But before he could put much distance between them, Jeff held up his hand. "Sorry, there's something I'm supposed to tell you."

Oliver stopped, his curiosity perking up at Jeff's words. "A message?"

"Yeah." Jeff frowned slightly, and Oliver could tell he was trying to recall the exact wording he was supposed to use. "Before he let me go, Vince told me that he had a warning for you. He said Ronald Spence says the Coltons need to stay out of his business, or else."

A chill raced down Oliver's spine at the mention of Ronald Spence. His older siblings, Morgan and Caleb, were investigating Spence as part of their efforts to right some of their father's wrongs. Ben Colton had taken a lot of bribes during his later years on the bench, and as a result, innocent people had been sent to jail. Several months ago, Ronald Spence had contacted the Truth Foundation, the organization established by his siblings in an effort to correct their father's misdeeds. Spence had claimed he was innocent of the drug charges that had put him in prison, and for a while, it seemed as though he was telling the truth. He'd been released from jail, freed after another man had confessed to the crimes. But more recent investigations indicated Spence wasn't a good guy after all. Oliver wasn't privy to the details of their investigation, but he knew his brother and sister had found evidence that, contrary to Spence's claims of innocence, he was really involved in smuggling drugs in Blue Larkspur.

Jeff's voice drew him out of his thoughts. "Does that make sense?" he asked, clearly not understanding the magnitude of the warning he'd just imparted.

Oliver swallowed and nodded, trying to look nonchalant. "Yes, it does." A chill skittered down his spine and he glanced reflexively at Hilary. Was she in danger now? What about the baby? He couldn't let anything happen to either one of them...

Jeff studied him for a few seconds. "Look, I know I'm kind of a mess right now. But if there's anything I can do to help you or your family, say the word."

Oliver's regard for Jeff increased a notch. "Thanks. Hopefully nothing will come of it."

Jeff nodded. "Offer stands." He walked over to his family, and after a brief exchange of words, he returned to cooking.

With the Westons distracted, Oliver stepped back into the dining area and pulled his phone from his pocket.

"Caleb Colton." His brother's voice was nononsense, his greeting professional.

"How did I know you'd still be at the office?" Oliver teased.

"Somebody's got to work for a living," Caleb replied, his tone warming as he recognized his brother. "Is Morgan with you?"

"Yeah, she's still in her office. What's up?"

"Can you grab her and put me on speaker? There's something I need to tell you."

"All right," Caleb replied. Oliver could hear his brother's curiosity, but Caleb's patience was legendary.

After a few seconds, Morgan's voice joined the conversation. "Oliver? What's going on?"

He could tell she was worried, so he started with reassurances to both of his lawyer siblings. "I'm fine. It's nothing to do with me." He quickly brought them up to speed on the situation with Jeff and Vince Doherty, then relayed the warning message from Spence.

"Maybe you two should consider slowing down," he said. "Who knows what this guy is capable of?"

"Not a chance," Morgan replied immediately. "Spence is bad news, and the fact that he's sending out warnings means we're starting to get to him."

"Agreed," Caleb said. "We helped set this guy free. We have to get him off the streets before more people get hurt."

Oliver sighed, knowing he was outnumbered. "I figured you two would say that. Just promise you'll be careful?" The last thing he needed was another sibling getting seriously injured; Ezra's shooting and subsequent surgery were more than enough for the family to handle.

"We'll be fine," Morgan said. "But thanks for the heads-up."

"I didn't know you were in town," Caleb said, changing the subject. "How long will you be here?"

"A while," Oliver said, not wanting to go into the details about his situation quite yet.

"Guess it's a family reunion," Morgan remarked dryly. "Gavin is here, too."

"Really?" That was surprising. His journalist brother rarely came to town for long—not even for Caleb's recent wedding. "Do you know why?"

Caleb sighed heavily. "He wants to focus on Dad and the Truth Foundation for an episode of his Crime Time podcast. He's especially interested in talking about Spence's case, and how it fits in with the overall mission of the foundation."

"Great," Oliver said sarcastically. "He couldn't have picked a better time."

"No kidding," said Morgan. "Caleb and I have talked to him repeatedly, asking him to postpone it. But he's determined to go ahead."

"Maybe Mom can get through to him," Oliver suggested.

"It's worth a shot," Caleb agreed.

Oliver ran a hand through his hair and turned slightly, just in time to see the door swing open behind him. Hilary poked her head into the dining area, clearly searching for him. He waved and she smiled, waiting for him to finish his call.

"Let me know if you need me for anything," Oliver said. "I can try to talk to Gavin if you think it will help." He lifted his arm in silent invitation and Hilary walked over to join him, slipping her arm around his waist.

"It might," Morgan said. "If we all ask him not to do this episode, he may actually listen."

Oliver chucked. "Have you met Gavin?"

After a few more minutes of chitchat, Oliver ended the call and turned his attention to Hilary. "Sorry about that," he said.

"Is everything okay?" She looked up at him with concern. "I saw your face when you and Jeff were talking. It looked like he said something that upset you."

"No, he just passed on a message for my family. I called Morgan and Caleb to let them know."

Hilary frowned. "I don't like the idea of you or your family having problems because you helped us."

"It's nothing to do with Jeff," Oliver assured her. She still looked doubtful, so he leaned down to press a kiss to the top of her head. "I promise."

"Okay," she said, apparently accepting his word. "Jeff is almost done with dinner. Are you getting hungry?"

At the mention of food, Oliver noticed the scents of warm garlic, sautéed onions and tomatoes in the air. His stomach rumbled in anticipation, and he had a flash of memory from dinners as a kid, the whole family gathered around the table laden with spaghetti and plates of garlic bread. The overlapping conversations, the laughter, the connections between everyone—he cherished those moments and looked forward to sharing them with his own child one day. "Definitely."

She smiled and steered them to the door to the kitchen. "Good. Because Jeff has fixed enough to feed an army."

Chapter 14

Hilary couldn't remember the last time she'd been this happy.

Her family was together. Her brother was home, mostly unscathed and in a far better mood.

And Oliver was by her side.

He fit right in with the family, easily engaging in conversation with her parents, trading jokes with her brother. It was like he'd always been there with them, rather than someone new they were still getting to know.

Her father opened a bottle of red wine and began to pour. Hilary held up her hand. "None for me, thanks."

Jeff looked at her, his expression questioning. "What? Are you okay?"

Like the rest of her family, Hilary normally enjoyed a glass with her meal. Her refusal had drawn attention, and she'd never been very good at lying...

She cast a quick glance at Oliver, who was trying to hide a smile. They'd all come together to celebrate Jeff's safe return. She might as well give them something else to be happy about.

"I'm fine," she told her brother. "But I won't be drinking any wine for a while. At least not until the baby is born."

Her father's jaw dropped open. "Baby?" he repeated, clearly shocked.

Hilary's mother laughed and dabbed at her eyes with a napkin. "You're pregnant!"

Everyone stood, hugging and laughing and talking over each other. Her parents congratulated her and Oliver, and even Jeff looked happy at the news that he was going to be an uncle.

"This is just wonderful," her mother said, once they had all taken their seats again. Her smile stretched from ear to ear as she glanced from Hilary to Oliver.

A sense of relief settled over Hilary as everyone chatted about baby names and nursery color schemes. It meant a lot to know her family supported her. The future held so many unknowns, but it was clear she wouldn't be facing them alone.

Jeff's food was delicious, as always. Hilary and

Oliver offered to help clean the kitchen after the meal, but her family insisted she get some rest. "It's been a stressful time for all of us," her father said. "Besides, your mother and I need to talk to Jeff."

"All right." Hilary let him walk her and Oliver to the door of the restaurant. "But, Dad, promise you won't keep me in the dark again. I know you were trying to handle Jeff's problems discreetly, but we're family. We need to stick together."

Her father pulled her in for a hug. "I see that now," he said. "Hopefully, nothing like this will ever happen again. But the next time we have a problem, we'll all talk about it together."

She nodded, releasing him so he could embrace Oliver. He said something near Oliver's ear, too soft for her to hear. Oliver smiled and shook his hand. "I will, sir," he replied.

Hilary waited until they were in the car before asking. "What did my dad say to you?"

Oliver smiled at her as he pulled out of the parking lot. "He wanted to make sure you're okay. He asked me to take care of you."

A sense of affectionate annoyance made her shake her head. "And you of course told him that I'm a grown woman who is fully capable of taking care of herself and the fact that I'm pregnant has not suddenly rendered me helpless?"

Oliver laughed. "Ah, something like that. Maybe not in so many words, but I think he got the gist of it."

He was quiet for the remainder of their drive back to the hotel. It was clear he was thinking about something, though she didn't know what. Had he and Jeff come to an arrangement regarding repayment? Was he rethinking his involvement with her now that he'd gotten to know her family a bit better? Or was he trying to figure out how to arrange his work to accommodate the baby?

Hilary wanted to give him the time and space he needed, but her curiosity eventually got the better of her patience. "Penny for your thoughts?" she asked as they rode the elevator to the penthouse.

Oliver glanced over and seemed to focus on her for the first time in a while. "Sorry about that," he said.

"It's fine," she told him as he opened the door to the suite. "I can tell you were going over something. Just wondering if it's anything I can help you with."

He shrugged. "Dinner tonight was really nice. The way you guys all sat around talking and joking with each other reminded me of the meals my family used to have, back when my dad was still alive."

"I bet your table was louder, though," Hilary said. "With fourteen people sitting together, I'm sure there were always a lot of separate conversations going on."

"For sure," Oliver agreed. "I generally sat with Dom and Ezra, but we mixed it up every once in a while."

"It sounds like you all were close."

"We were." Oliver sat on the sofa in the living room area and Hilary took the spot next to him. "Part of it was just being around each other all the time, but we all liked each other, too."

"Sounds like your mom did a great job after your dad died." She shook her head. "I can't imagine having twelve kids as a single parent. That must have been an unbelievable amount of work for her."

"Looking back, I'm not sure how she did it," Oliver replied. "While my dad was alive, they somehow managed to give each one of us some one-on-one time, so we never felt lost in the shuffle. And then, once he died and everything went to hell, she still showed all of us so much love."

"Maybe your mom can give me some parenting tips," Hilary joked. Her own family was close, but she wouldn't turn down advice from a woman who had raised a dozen children.

"You're going to be an amazing mother," Oliver said. "I'm sure of it."

"Well, that makes one of us," Hilary replied lightly. "Because I'm definitely worried."

He placed his hand on her knee, his touch warm and comforting. "You're going to make a wonderful mother," he said. "You're smart, kind, funny. You're patient and creative. And you have a strong sense of right and wrong. This baby will be lucky to have you."

His words helped quiet the voice of her worries. "I know you're going to be a great dad, too," she said.

Oliver's mouth twisted. "I don't know. I'm impatient, somewhat reckless and I spend too much time at my job. I'm also not great at talking about my feelings."

Hilary couldn't help but laugh. "I'd noticed. But you're also loyal, thoughtful and you'd do anything for the people you care about. What was your relationship like with your dad?"

He didn't answer right away. "It was good," he said finally. "At least until we learned about his misconduct…" he trailed off, shaking his head. "In some ways, that was even harder than his death. It's like I thought I knew him but found out I didn't. Not really. He led a double life—the doting father at home, the model judge in public. But he actually was the corrupt official in private, happy to accept bribes and subvert justice for his own financial gain—and ruin so many lives. The fact that he was able to lie so easily made me wonder if he'd been lying with us, too? After he died in that car crash, all my memories with him were tainted by the idea that my dad hadn't really loved us, that he'd just been playing the part because that was what was expected of him."

Hilary's heart broke for him, and the young man he'd once been. "I don't think that's true," she said softly. "I know I never met your dad, but surely he and your mom wouldn't have had such a big family if they didn't love each one of you?"

Oliver shrugged. "Who can say? It's not like my

mom would ever tell us. Hell, maybe he even had her fooled as well."

"I don't believe that," she declared. "I know your dad did horrible things, but it sounds to me like he still loved his kids."

"So you're saying that makes it okay?" He looked surprised, and she realized he'd misunderstood what she was trying to say.

Hilary shook her head. "Absolutely not. I'm not trying to excuse his choices. I just think the real man was the one who loved his family. He became corrupt not because it was his true nature, but because he wanted to give you all the world, and that was the only way he could see to do it."

"Maybe so," Oliver replied. "But what if I have those same traits? You said it yourself—I take care of the people who are important to me. Aren't you a little bit worried I could turn into my father?"

"No." She didn't have to think about it. "I know that won't happen."

She saw the doubt in his eyes and knew she had to do better. "Look, I'm not saying you won't make mistakes. We both will. But if you were going to lie and cheat, you would be doing it already in your business. The fact that you're not tells me everything I need to know about you."

Oliver sighed. "You make some good points," he allowed. "You could be right."

"I am," Hilary said confidently. "I know you're

smart enough to learn from your father's history. And from the mistakes you've made yourself."

He smiled. "Dom and Ezra would waste no time setting me straight if I hadn't."

"That, too," Hilary said. "Between me and your brothers, you don't have to worry."

"I don't know," Oliver replied, a glint of humor in his eyes. "I did make a deal with a loan shark today. What if that was the first step down a slippery slope of depravity and illegal activity?"

Hilary laughed and pressed a quick kiss to his mouth. "Then we'll roll down that hill together."

Tuesday

Oliver couldn't remember the last time he'd slept so well.

Maybe it was the aftereffects of talking to Hilary last night. They'd chatted well into the night, talking about their families and childhoods, their hopes and dreams for this baby. Then they'd made love again, this time slowly, savoring every touch, every sigh. He'd fallen asleep with Hilary in his arms, and he'd woken with the scent of her in his nose and her warmth pressed against him.

He'd never felt so…settled. So at peace. Normally, there was an inner sense of turmoil, a swirl of dissatisfaction in his chest that propelled him forward, forcing him to keep moving, keep working. He never rested for long, and when he did, there was always a little voice in the back of his mind questioning his lack of action.

But with Hilary, things were different. That inner voice was silenced, and he didn't feel the need to push ahead just for the sake of moving. Simply being with her was enough.

He glanced over at her as they walked, hand in hand. Last night she had mentioned wanting to check out some of the baby stores in Blue Larkspur. He'd seen a boutique near the center of town and figured it was a good place to start.

Hilary looked lighter somehow, now that the stress of Jeff's situation had been lifted. The spark was back in her eyes, and her shoulders no longer slumped with the weight of her worries. She practically glowed and, based on the number of glances she'd been getting as they walked, Oliver knew he wasn't the only one who thought she was beautiful.

"Are you sure about this?" she asked as they approached the storefront. "It looks really expensive in there."

Oliver squeezed her hand. "Of course I'm sure. If it makes you feel any better, we're not going to buy out the store. But it will be nice to take a look around and start a list of things we'll need once the baby arrives. We can always talk to my sister Rachel and get the scoop on the things we'll really need and the stuff that's a waste of money."

"Okay," Hilary said. Little did she know he planned to spare no expense when it came to providing for the baby. But that was a discussion for another time.

A bell chimed softly as they walked through the heavy door. An older woman greeted them with a smile and an offer of help, fading into the background when Oliver told her they were just browsing.

The place smelled faintly of baby powder. Several round tables were placed throughout the store, displaying merchandise. Clothes hung on the walls, and several nursery models were set up in the back of the store.

Oliver blinked, feeling like a deer in headlights. He'd never before been confronted with so much baby stuff, and it was a bit overwhelming to see it all in one place. Would they really need all of this gear?

Beside him, he heard Hilary take a deep breath. "Well," she said softly. "Where should we begin?"

Oliver glanced around and made an executive decision. "Furniture," he declared. "The kid is going to need a place to sleep."

They made their way through various displays until they reached the nursery models. At first glance, everything looked pretty much the same. But after studying the different models carefully, he began to notice differences among the cribs and dressers and changing tables and recliners and...

"There's so much to choose from," Hilary said, sounding about as overwhelmed as he felt.

"Yeah," he agreed. "Do you see any that catch your eye?"

She surveyed the closest models critically, making a little humming noise as she walked past each display. Then she let out a soft gasp and darted off to the side.

Oliver caught up with her after she stopped in front of a crib. Even he had to admit it was a pretty one, the mahogany wood carved in smooth, graceful lines. There was a matching dresser and recliner to complete the set. As soon as he saw Hilary's face, he knew this was the one she wanted.

"It's so pretty," she said, running her hand along the top edge of the crib. "And look—it converts into a toddler bed and then a twin-size bed later!"

"Very nice," he agreed. Oliver didn't care what the crib looked like as long as it was safe, but he wasn't going to take away from Hilary's joy. She reached for the price tag but he placed his hand over hers, stopping her.

"Don't worry about it," he said. "Remember, I'm taking care of this stuff." It was considerate of her to consider the price, but he didn't want her to settle for something simply because it was less expensive. After she'd had to deal with silence from him, splurging on baby stuff was the least he could do.

She bit her lip and nodded. Oliver glanced around and caught the sales lady's eye. She darted over and he gestured to the crib and dresser. "We'd like to order these, please."

"Of course," she replied. "The rocking chair, too?"

He looked over to find Hilary seated in the chair,

her eyes closed as she settled back into the cushions. "Yes," he replied. "The whole set." They could send it to Hilary's apartment for now, while they figured out their long-term living situation. It would be great to get a place big enough for the two—soon to be three—of them, but he didn't want to rush Hilary by suggesting they move in together just yet.

"Excellent choices. I'll start writing this up. Would you like to continue to look around?"

"Yes, we'll do that," Oliver replied. The nursery furniture was only part of what they would need. They might as well look around for the rest of it.

Hilary got to her feet and walked over to him. "I wish you'd let me pay for some of this," she muttered as he led her to the display of car seats.

For the next hour, they selected baby gear: a car seat, a stroller, a swing. He insisted on picking out a high chair, though Hilary resisted.

"The baby won't be able to use it for months!"

"Doesn't matter," he replied. "I like to be prepared."

Feeling like they'd made a good start, Oliver walked to the register and waited while the saleslady rang up all their purchases. Hilary wandered over to a display of infant dresses, a small smile on her face as she ran her hand over the soft fabrics. She pulled a pale pink dress from the rack, admiring the tiny roses embroidered along the collar.

Oliver's phone buzzed in his pocket and he answered without taking his eyes off Hilary. It was hard to believe that they would soon be dressing a new-born, possibly in that very outfit. An image flashed in his mind of her holding up their infant, cooing up at her as their little daughter smiled.

Then the voice in his ear crashed into his fantasy, bringing him back to earth. "We're ready for the next installment."

Oliver tore his gaze away from Hilary and retreated a few steps away from the register. "What? Who is this?"

"Never mind that. You made a deal with Mr. Doherty yesterday."

"I did," Oliver acknowledged, tightening his grip on the phone. "And the agreement was I'd pay the next bit in a week."

"The schedule has changed." The man's voice was hard and inflexible. "Now you're going to pay him tomorrow."

Oliver's stomach sank and he realized his brothers had been right—bargaining with Vince Doherty may have gotten Jeff back, but now Oliver himself was on the hook. "That wasn't our agreement."

"It is now And go ahead and double the amount, to make up for your attitude."

Heat flashed through Oliver's body as his temper spiked. "Who the hell do you think you are?"

"I'm the guy you don't mess with," the man replied. "And if you miss this payment, I'll be happy to take something else you value."

Oliver sucked in a breath and the man continued.

"That dress looks real nice. Pink is definitely your girl's color."

Oliver immediately looked across the store and spied Hilary standing by the front windows, holding up another pink baby dress. A chill raced over his skin and the blood drained from his head as he realized they were being watched.

He crossed the store in three strides and grabbed her arm. She let out a yelp as he practically dragged her deeper into the store, away from the windows. A harsh, mocking laugh erupted from his phone. "Don't even think about touching her," Oliver growled.

"Call me at this number when you've got the money," the man said, his tone amused. "I'll give you instructions for the drop-off then."

Oliver ended the call and put his phone back into his pocket. Hilary stared up at him with wide eyes and he felt a spike of guilt for scaring her. "What's going on?"

"We have to go," he said, wondering if there was a back door to this place and if so, the odds that the saleswoman would let them use it. "Now."

Chapter 15

Hilary waited until they were back at the hotel before demanding answers.

It was clear something was wrong, based on the way Oliver had grabbed her at the store. Her feet had barely touched the floor as he'd pulled her away from the windows, but he'd refused to answer any questions while they were still in public. He'd quickly paid for their items, shelling out extra to have them delivered. Then he'd insisted they leave through the back of the store, brooking no argument from the flustered shop employee who seemed just as confused as Hilary regarding Oliver's sudden change in behavior.

Once they'd made it to the car, Oliver had taken

off almost as soon as he'd closed his door. He'd spent the drive back to the hotel on the phone, calling Dom and then Ezra.

"What is going on?" she said, turning to face him after stepping into the entryway of the suite. "One minute, we're picking out baby stuff and everything is fine, the next you're dragging me across the store and we're sneaking out the back."

"I'll explain everything," he promised. "Ezra will be here soon and then I'll tell you what happened."

She pressed her lips together, knowing it was futile to push him. Something had spooked Oliver, badly enough to change his entire mood. He was normally calm and composed, but now he paced the suite with nervous energy, his brows drawn together in a frown.

Frustration built in her chest as she watched him. Why wouldn't he talk to her? They were supposed to be partners, yet he was keeping things from her. How could they have a relationship if he didn't share his thoughts and feelings?

"I don't like it when you shut me out," she said quietly.

Oliver stopped pacing and turned to face her. "I'm not trying to keep secrets from you. I just want to wait until Ezra gets here so I only have to tell this story once."

"Fair enough." She could be patient a bit longer, if it was that important to him. Still, a small part of her wondered if she'd ever be on equal footing with

Oliver's brothers. Whenever something came up, it seemed like Oliver's first response was to call his fellow triplets. Would there ever come a time when she was the person he turned to for advice or help?

Fortunately, they didn't have to wait long. There was a loud knock on the door, and Oliver opened it for his brother.

Hilary hadn't seen Ezra in a while, and never outside of the restaurant. But there was something about him that put her at ease. The brothers were the same height, but while Oliver was lean, Ezra was muscular. His light brown hair was trimmed short, making her think of a military cut that was a little on the long side. He had blue eyes like Oliver, but instead of Oliver's easygoing, lighthearted demeanor, Ezra seemed quiet and serious.

He stepped inside, moving with the confidence of a man who was used to giving orders and having them obeyed. He clapped Oliver on the shoulder, pulling him in for a one-armed hug. Then he looked at Hilary and smiled.

The expression transformed his face, revealing a softer side to this strong man. He walked over and reached for her, drawing her in for a gentle hug. "Congratulations," he said quietly. "How are you feeling?"

There was a genuine note of concern in his voice, making it clear he wasn't asking the question simply to be polite. "I'm okay," Hilary replied, touched by his thoughtfulness.

"That's good." Ezra looked down at her. "If you need anything or want to talk to someone about your pregnancy, Theresa would be happy to chat. The girls are six now, but she still remembers what it was like."

"Not to mention Rachel," said Oliver. "Iris is what, nearly a year now?" He glanced at Ezra for confirmation, and his brother nodded.

"That sounds right. We Coltons definitely have experience with babies."

Hilary laughed, appreciating the offer. "That would be nice," she said. "Maybe after Oliver tells us what's going on?"

Oliver gestured for them to proceed him into the living room, and they all took seats.

"Do you want to wait for your brother?" she asked.

Oliver shook his head. "Dom is coming in from Denver. Said we could start without him."

"I got a call today," he continued, describing their shopping trip and the phone call that had interrupted things. When he got to the part about the man describing the dress she'd been looking at, Hilary's blood ran cold.

"Oh my God," she said, her stomach churning. Never in a million years had she thought she might come to the attention of the loan shark. After all, she'd had nothing to do with her brother's debts or Oliver's deal to pay them off.

"I won't let anyone hurt you," Oliver said, his voice brooking no argument. "Please believe me when I say I'll do anything to keep you and the baby safe."

Ezra nodded, voicing reassurances as well. Still, Hilary couldn't help but wonder how the brothers could be so sure? She had a life, a job. Errands to run, friends to see. She couldn't stay locked up in this hotel suite forever.

Besides, even if Oliver paid the man, she didn't think Doherty was ever going to stop. He'd bleed Oliver dry, using threats against her as a way to make him comply. And when Oliver ran out of money? What then? Would he come after her or her parents next? They only had so much to give…

"I should have never let you pay Jeff's debt." Tears welled in her eyes and her throat grew tight. She'd been so focused on getting her brother back she hadn't thought through the consequences of Oliver's actions. Instead of solving one problem, they'd created more.

"It was the only way," Oliver replied. "We had to get your brother released before they hurt him. I'm not sorry for making that deal. I'm only sorry you're now in Doherty's sights." He reached over and took her hand. "I'm going to fix this," he promised.

She wanted to take comfort from his touch, but her thoughts were spinning out of control. She had enjoyed shopping with Oliver earlier. Picking out baby stuff together had made her feel closer to him. But now that she knew they had been spied on the whole time, she felt violated. What other moments had that man witnessed? Had he stood in the darkness last night, peering through the windows of the restaurant while she and Oliver dined with her family? Had he seen the joy on her parents' faces after she announced her pregnancy? And later, when she and Oliver had left. Had he watched them embrace, seen them kiss before getting into the car?

Would they ever have privacy again, or would they be forever subject to surveillance by Doherty's men?

Unable to sit still, Hilary stood.

"I need some air," she announced.

Oliver looked like he wanted to protest, but Ezra sent his brother a warning glance. "Understandable," Ezra said. "But please stay inside the suite."

Hilary nodded, having no intention of leaving. She retreated to the bedroom and began to pace, needing an outlet for the nervous energy running through her body.

Should she call her parents? Warn them they might be targets, too?

No. That would only worry them, and her mother was still recovering from the strain of Jeff's kidnapping. If she learned Hilary was now in danger, she might go over the edge.

Hilary forced herself to take deep breaths, trying to fight off a looming sense of powerlessness. There might not be anything she could do from this hotel room, but she wasn't going to be a passive victim.

She'd let Oliver and his brother talk, and then she'd insist they call the police.

No more messing around, trying to solve this problem on their own. It was time to get the authorities involved. They wouldn't be safe until Doherty was behind bars.

Ezra waited until Hilary left the room. Then he glanced over at Oliver. "Should I say 'I told you so' now, or later?"

Oliver glared at his older-by-minutes brother. "Never works for me."

Ezra shook his head. "We warned you. And now you're really in it."

Irritation flared in Oliver's chest. "Yes." No sense in trying to deny it. "Are you going to help me, or do I have to figure this out on my own?"

Ezra's blue gaze was steady. "I'm here, aren't I?"

Oliver glanced down, feeling bad for lashing out. "You are. I'm sorry—this isn't your fault and I shouldn't take it out on you."

"It's all right," Ezra replied easily. "I know you're stressed. If someone threatened Theresa or the girls, I'd be a wreck, too."

"How are they?" Oliver asked. A small part of him was still adjusting to the fact that his brother had found someone. Ezra had always been a bit of a loner, but settling down with Theresa and her twin daughters had changed him, revealing new sides of his personality that Oliver hadn't appreciated before.

"They're good," Ezra said, his mouth curving in the smile he reserved for any mention of "his girls," as he called the three of them.

"Did you mean it?" Oliver asked. "Would Theresa really be willing to talk to Hilary?" He knew Hilary was still adjusting to the news of the pregnancy; she had to have questions about what to expect in the coming weeks and months, and seeing as how he had no direct experience, Oliver wasn't going to be much help in that department. It would be nice if Hilary could talk to Theresa or Rachel, not only to get her questions answered but to get to know more of his family as well.

"Of course," Ezra said. "She told me to mention it the next time I saw you."

"That's sweet of her." His brother had lucked out in the romance department. Both of them had, really—he couldn't have picked better women for Ezra and Dom than Theresa and Sami.

And as for himself? He'd hit the jackpot, too.

Now, he just had to keep her safe.

"Let's hear it," Ezra said, changing the subject.

"Hear what?" Oliver frowned, not following his brother's line of thought.

Ezra sighed and leaned forward, placing his elbows on his knees. "Go ahead and tell me your plan to deal with Doherty. Get it out of the way so we can come up with something that will actually work."

That stung a little, but his brother had a point. Oliver's original approach hadn't exactly worked out.

"I don't really have a plan," he said. "That's why I called you and Dom. I was hoping we could come up with something together." He hated having to ask his siblings for help, especially so soon after they'd already backed him up. But his worry for Hilary and the safety of their baby outweighed the demands of his pride. He'd grovel before his brothers for the rest of his life as long as she was safe.

Ezra was quiet a moment, clearly thinking. Finally, he leaned back against the sofa. "I don't want to speak for Dom, but I think we need to bring in the police. The only way this guy is going to leave you alone is if he's arrested and put behind bars. Otherwise, he'll keep demanding more money and increasing his threats to get you to comply."

"Agreed." Oliver had already figured out Doherty wasn't going to go away without a fight. The problem was, he wasn't sure the Blue Larkspur PD—in particular, Chief Lawson,—would be too happy to learn he'd bargained with the man to facilitate Jeff's release.

"I can contact the officers assigned to Jeff's initial case," he continued. "I'm not sure they'll help me, though. I didn't tell them about my deal with Vince. The cops might be mad that I kept them out of the loop." From what he'd seen, Officer Simpkins didn't seem the type to forgive and forget. Would he or his boss be willing to help now?

"That's definitely possible," Ezra said. "But I bet a little friendly pressure from the FBI and a word from the district attorney would grease some wheels in that regard. Besides, a guy like this? I'd be shocked if the police didn't already have a file started on him."

"I hadn't thought of that." It made sense, though. Doherty wasn't exactly a model citizen. His activities and association with Ronald Spence were proof of that. If the police were already looking into him, and if he could supply additional evidence against him, Rachel would probably jump at the chance to file charges and get this guy off the street. Now he just had to set the wheels in motion and get everyone on board...

"Uh-oh." Ezra's voice interrupted his thoughts. "I recognize that look. What are you planning, little brother?"

"Just a simple sting operation," Oliver replied, his mood starting to lift as the details came together in his mind. "Here's what I need you to do..."

Wednesday

Hilary slept badly. Again.

After stepping out of the room while Ezra and Oliver talked, she'd calmed down enough to curl up on the bed. The next thing she knew, Oliver was shaking her awake, asking if she was hungry.

"I think we should go to the police."

He'd smiled at that and explained he already had. "Simpkins and his partner are on the case now," he'd said, telling her that his sister Rachel, the district attorney, was getting involved as well. "She's excited about this case. Apparently, they've wanted to go after Doherty for a while."

Hilary had accepted his words at face value, and they'd had a light meal. But as Oliver talked, she couldn't shake the feeling that he was holding something back.

"Is there anything else you want to tell me?" she'd asked.

"No, everything is fine," he'd answered. "I'm just ready to get this behind us, so we can move on with our lives."

She'd fallen asleep in his arms, but hadn't stayed that way for long. Instead, she found herself pacing the living room of the suite, worried but unable to articulate why.

The fact that the authorities were involved in the blackmail situation should have calmed her. On some level, it did.

But she knew Oliver Colton. And he wouldn't be satisfied letting someone else handle his business.

He found her on the sofa in the morning.

"Babe, what's going on? Why are you out here?"

Hilary smiled faintly. "I had trouble sleeping. Too many naps lately."

He sat next to her, his sleep-warm body radiating heat like a furnace. "You'll need another one today to catch up." He lifted his arm, drawing her against his side.

Hilary relaxed against him with a sigh. In the

light of day, some of her midnight fears seemed overblown. "You're not going to do anything, right?"

"About Vince?" Oliver ran his hand down the length of her arm. "I'm going to let the police do their job."

"I don't want you to be in any danger," she continued. They'd talked about this before, after his first meeting with the loan shark. But she wanted to remind him that he'd agreed not to go off on his own anymore.

"Like I said, I'm going to let the police handle it."

They sat together for a few minutes, enjoying the silence and each other's company. Finally, Oliver spoke again. "Do you still want to check out the ranch today?"

Yesterday, Oliver had mentioned a visit to Gemini Ranch, the operation owned and run by two of his siblings, twins Jasper and Aubrey. Ezra had mentioned Theresa and the girls would be there today, and Oliver had suggested Hilary hang out there while he spoke to the police about Doherty.

"Yes, I'd like to see it and meet more of your family."

His cheek rested on the top of her head and she felt him smile. "They're going to be so excited," he said. "And I know the girls are going to love you. They'll be thrilled to learn about the baby. You should see the way they adore Iris."

Hilary's mood brightened at the prospect of spending time with more of Oliver's siblings and getting to know Theresa and her daughters. Last night, Oliver had told her it was only a matter of time before Ezra proposed. Even though she didn't know if marriage was in the cards for her and Oliver, it was nice to think about the fact that their baby would grow up with several kids around.

"Are you sure your brother and sister won't mind my being there?" From what she'd been told, Gemini Ranch was a busy place. She hated to add to their work, especially on such short notice.

"I'm positive," Oliver reassured her. "I talked to Aubrey last night, and she said the more, the merrier. You can watch the cattle drive with Theresa and her twins."

"All right," Hilary replied. "What time am I supposed to go?"

"I have an appointment at the police station at ten, so I figured I'd drop you off at nine thirty? Ezra said that's about the time Theresa will be there. The girls love feeding the horses and Aubrey always has some extra carrots in her pockets."

"That sounds like fun." It actually did. She couldn't remember the last time she'd spent a day outside or been around kids and animals. And while she wanted to stay with Oliver and be there while he talked to the police, it was probably better for her anxiety if she didn't listen to all the details of the threat against her.

A few hours later, after breakfast and a shower, they pulled up to the main ranch house. Oliver parked and rounded the hood of the car to offer his hand as she climbed out. Together, they walked hand in hand up the steps and through the large wooden doors.

Hilary gasped as they stepped inside. The place was huge, with lofted ceilings, shining wood floors and a wall of windows at the far end that looked out over the property.

"Oliver!" She turned at the sound of a woman's voice. A blonde, curvy woman in glasses walked toward them, a broad smile on her face. She threw her arms around Oliver and hugged him tightly. "It's about time you stopped by!"

"Hey, sis." He returned her embrace, smiling fondly. "Good to see you."

Aubrey released him, then turned to Hilary. "Hi," she said, sticking out her hand. "You must be Hilary."

Hilary shook her hand, nodding. "It's nice to meet you. Thanks for letting me come out today."

"Of course!" Aubrey took Hilary's arm and led her to a long table, indicating the coffee samovars and pitchers of ice water and iced tea.

Hilary sipped water while Oliver and Aubrey chatted for a few minutes, their conversation equal parts teasing insults and catching up. She liked seeing him with his siblings, watching the easy banter he had with them, the way they jumped between reminiscing over shared memories and current events. It was clear the Coltons were close, and while the idea of being a part of this large family was a bit intimidating, she knew they would all rally around her baby.

Both Aubrey and Oliver made it a point to include her, and Aubrey was especially chatty and welcoming. Hilary's earlier nerves about being left here with relative strangers faded, and by the time Oliver had to go to meet the police, she felt as though she and Aubrey were on the road to becoming friends.

She walked him to the door of the lodge and hugged him. "Let me know how it goes," she said. "Hopefully the police will be able to do something with the information you have for them."

"I think they will." Oliver sounded confident. "I'll be back in a few hours and we won't have to worry about this guy ever again." He leaned down and kissed her. "I love you," he said softly, holding her gaze.

Hilary started to melt. If they'd been alone, she would have led him to the bedroom to show him how much those words meant to her. "I love you, too." Would she ever get tired of hearing him say that?

She watched him walk to the car and waved goodbye as he started to drive away. She felt a presence at her side and turned to find Aubrey standing next to her. "He'll be okay," she said kindly. "If there's one thing I know about my brother, it's that he always finds a way out of trouble."

Hilary smiled at that, hoping she was right and that Oliver's luck hadn't finally run out.

"Come on," Aubrey said, beckoning her back inside the lodge. "Theresa and the girls will be here in a few minutes. Let's get loaded up on carrots and apples for the horses."

Chapter 16

In terms of plans, it wasn't the safest.

Oliver jolted along the gravel road that led to Vince Doherty's warehouse, his mind spinning with what-ifs and worry. When he'd agreed to serve as bait during this sting operation, it had seemed like a good idea. The police had made it sound like this was the only way to get the evidence they needed to arrest Vince. They'd promised to be right behind him, waiting in the wings to swoop in and take Doherty and his band of thugs down at the first hint of trouble.

But as Oliver hit another pothole that made his teeth rattle, he had to wonder if he'd made a mistake.

The police said they'd be around, but a quick glance in the rearview mirror confirmed he was the only one on this road. Sure, maybe the cops were hanging back so as not to be seen by Doherty's guys, but in this moment, Oliver would have appreciated some reassurance.

The skin of his chest itched where Simpkins had taped the microphone. As predicted, the officer wasn't happy to learn about Oliver's deal with Doherty. But Ezra's suggestion to involve Rachel had put a spring in the step of the Blue Larkspur PD. As soon as she'd confirmed she was ready to file charges, the police had been all too happy to put together a takedown of Vince's operation. Oliver had hoped his evidence of blackmail would be enough, but Rachel had explained it would be too easy for Doherty to dodge that charge.

"We need to get him for something bigger," she'd said yesterday, when Oliver had called for advice. "If you can get him to admit to kidnapping Jeff, that would be a start."

And so Oliver had agreed to go back into the lion's den. Hilary would hate it, but it had to be done.

Dom and Ezra were in the area, but they hadn't told him where.

"We've got your back, little brother." Dom had hugged him, his expression serious.

"Don't do anything stupid," Ezra had advised.

Officer Simpkins had been the last one to talk to him before he'd started this drive. "Get him talking as much as you can. But don't be too pushy about it or he'll know something's up. Remember your code word if things go south?"

"Spaghetti."

"Good. We'll come running, but it will take a few minutes. Try not to get killed in the meantime."

The advice hadn't done much to calm Oliver's nerves. He couldn't stand the thought of leaving his baby without a father, abandoning Hilary to do everything alone. Still, what choice did he have? If the police didn't get Doherty and his enforcers off the street, he'd never get out from under the man's thumb. He couldn't risk Hilary or their baby, not when it was in his power to do something.

The thought of her sent a prickle of guilt down his spine. They'd talked before about his tendency to act first and talk to her about it later. But if he'd shared this plan with her, it would have caused her so much stress. Her body was still healing from the attack and her emotions were leveling out after Jeff's return. The last thing he wanted to do was burden her again, especially since her worry wouldn't have any effect on the outcome of this plan.

No, better for him to handle this on his own. She was safe at the ranch with his siblings and Theresa and her girls. Knowing that, he could focus on the task at hand and get it over with.

He pulled up to the warehouse. There was a different guy on watch this time. He approached the car quickly, his hand on the door before Oliver could fully stand.

"Easy there," Oliver said, holding up his hands to show he wasn't a threat. "I'm just here to talk to the boss."

"What's your name?" The man eyed him up and down, his stance aggressive. He was clearly itching for a fight, but Oliver wasn't about to give him an excuse.

"Oliver Colton. I have a payment."

The guy relaxed a bit at that. "All right," he said. "Come on."

Oliver shut the car door and took a step forward, following Doherty's guard. The guy took a few steps, then whirled around and started a rough pat down.

Oliver held his breath, hoping against hope the man wouldn't feel the thin wire and small mic taped to his chest. It had seemed so tiny when Simpkins had placed it on him, but now that this guy was pawing at him, it felt huge.

After an endless moment, the man turned and gestured for Oliver to follow him again. Oliver let out a sigh and began to walk, his knees still a little wobbly.

Doherty stared at him as he entered the office. "Mr. Colton," he said. "I wasn't aware we had an appointment today." He cut a murderous glare at the guard, who went pale.

"Really?" Oliver replied, trying to sound casual. "I received a call yesterday, telling me you wanted another payment today."

Doherty didn't respond and Oliver felt a flare of

panic. How was he supposed to get Doherty to incriminate himself if the man refused to talk?

"My associate should have given you instructions on where to go," Vince said, his voice tight.

Oliver shook his head. "I don't deal with middlemen." He pulled an envelope of cash from his back pocket and thumped it on Doherty's desk. "If you want something, do me the courtesy of telling me yourself. And don't ever threaten my family again."

Doherty held his gaze, a calculating gleam in his eyes. "I believe there's been a misunderstanding."

"Which part?" Oliver challenged. "Are you saying your thug didn't call and demand another payment? Or that he didn't threaten my family on your behalf?"

"I was under the impression Ms. Weston is not related to you," Doherty replied smoothly. "Are you saying she is?"

Oliver's hands clenched and the urge to hit Doherty rose in his chest. His emotions must have shown on his face, because Doherty smiled. "Careful there, Mr. Colton. I'd hate for you to do anything rash."

"Why's that?" Oliver goaded. He just needed to get Vince to admit to something! Then he could get out of here and let the police take over. "You gonna kidnap me the way you did Jeff?"

Doherty's expression was smug. "I'm sure I don't know what you're talking about."

"You know they're on film, right? The guys who

broke into the restaurant? The police have pictures of their faces."

Doherty's smile faded, but he didn't reply.

"I wonder how long it will take to find them?" Oliver mused. "Blue Larkspur isn't that big. And guys like that, I'm sure they've already got a rap sheet. I bet they'll sing like canaries to avoid a long sentence."

Vince looked uncomfortable now, and Oliver knew he'd hit a nerve. He leaned forward, placing his hands on the desk. "What do you think they'll say about you?"

"Enough." Doherty's voice was cold. "I found you entertaining at first, but now you just annoy me."

"Fine with me," Oliver said. "Consider this your last payment. We're done here." He moved as if to leave, but Doherty spoke again.

"Is that what you think?"

Oliver turned back to find the man staring at him incredulously, a strange gleam in his eyes. He laughed, but there was no humor in the sound. "Please. We're done when I say we're done. Let's get one thing straight here—you are not in charge. I am. You belong to me now. And I am going to bleed you dry. Once that's done, I'll go after your pretty little girlfriend and her family. And then I'll blackmail every single one of your family members until there's nothing left. And I'm not the only one with the resources to go against your family. I assume you got my message about Spence?"

A black rage coursed through Oliver's body. Before he knew what was happening, he lunged across the desk and punched Doherty in the middle of his self-satisfied face.

Vince let out a yelp as Oliver's fist made contact. His nose crunched under Oliver's knuckles, and a shock traveled up his arm. He drew back to hit Doherty again, but before he could land another blow, the guard grabbed him and yanked him away.

"I told you to leave my family alone." His breath came in great heaves, his body still on the edge of violence.

Doherty cupped his nose and glared at Oliver. "Take him out back," he instructed the guard. "Get rid of him. No one touches me and lives to talk about it."

The man began to drag Oliver out. "You're going to kill me?" Oliver yelled. "What about your money? You can't get cash from a dead man."

Doherty walked over and got in his face. "You're more valuable to me dead right now. And I'll still get my money. I'm sure your girl will see to that."

Oliver tried to grab him again, but the guard pinned his arms behind his back. Doherty's grin was bloody. "Make it hurt," he instructed as the guard pulled Oliver away.

"What should I do when I'm done?" the man asked.

"Dump his body in the woods," Vince instructed. "The animals will take care of the rest."

Several muscular guys approached, apparently having heard the commotion. "Come on," said the guard holding him. "Time to have some fun."

He marched Oliver through a door that led to the back side of the warehouse. A line of trees started about fifty feet away, and there was no road here or any nearby buildings. The place was isolated, and as the men circled around him, Oliver felt a visceral pang of fear.

How long would it take for the police to arrive? Were they coming already, or did he need to alert them? Better make sure they knew he needed help.

"Hey, guys," he said, eyeing each of the men as they moved around him. "This is just a big misunderstanding. Let's go grab some lunch and talk it over. You like spaghetti? I love spaghetti. Spaghetti is my favorite."

One of the men frowned. "Shut up."

Oliver's jaw exploded in pain as someone hit him. The blow had come so fast he hadn't anticipated it, and he dropped to his knees as blackness threatened to take over his vision.

He felt rather than saw movement around him and forced himself to stand. If he dropped to the ground it would be all over. He wasn't going to give these bastards the satisfaction of taking him out that easily.

Oliver shook his head to distract himself from the pain. He managed to dodge another blow, but someone hit him from behind, planting a fist in his side.

He lunged away but tripped over a rock and found himself on his back, staring up at the sky.

Someone kicked him, but his mind was no longer on the pain of the beating. Hilary's face flashed before him and his heart broke with the knowledge that he wouldn't see her again or meet their baby. Guilt stole his breath as he realized she'd see this as a betrayal, when the truth was, he'd done it to protect her. And at least he'd done that—Doherty had ordered his murder in clear terms. There was no way he'd avoid jail time for that.

There was another kick, this time to his legs. The circle of men contracted around him and Oliver braced himself, knowing the end was close. Then suddenly the men stepped back, and to Oliver's amazement, some of them started running.

The wail of sirens cut through the ringing in Oliver's ears. From somewhere close by, a voice boomed from a megaphone. "This is the police. We have you surrounded."

Oliver tried to sit up, but his body protested the movement so he stayed where he was. Dom and Ezra found him a few minutes later, staring up at the sky with one eye swollen shut, and he knew his bloodied mouth was arranged in a wide grin of satisfaction.

Hilary was helping the girls feed treats to the horses when one of them let out a squeal of delight.

"Ezra!"

Neve and Claire took off like rabbits, two blond

ponytails bouncing as they raced across the field to tackle Ezra. Hilary smiled as she watched him stop and embrace the twins, crouching down so he could hug them both.

She glanced at Theresa and saw the love on her face as she looked at her daughters and her man. Hilary felt a pang of longing mixed with hope—that would be her and Oliver one day, with their child.

Ezra straightened and started walking toward them, the girls flanking him. Hilary had initially thought he'd come to visit Theresa and the twins, but as he approached, she could tell by the look on his face that something was wrong.

Oliver.

Something must have happened to him. Why else would his brother be approaching now, staring at her with pity in his eyes?

Hilary's heart started to pound and her palms began to sweat. She wiped them on her pants and reached for her phone. No missed calls. Apparently, this news needed to be delivered in person.

Her imagination kicked into overdrive. Had he been in a car accident on the way to the police station? Had something happened to him once he'd arrived? Maybe Doherty's thugs had grabbed him before he could talk to the cops? Where was he? Why hadn't he called her?

Panic built inside her, making her throat tight. Her emotions must have shown on her face, because as soon as Ezra walked up, he reached out to steady her.

"He's okay."

Hilary swayed a bit on her feet. If Oliver was fine, why did Ezra look so serious?

"There's been an accident. He's at the hospital."

Tears welled in her eyes as she stared up at Ezra. "What happened?"

Ezra shook his head slightly. "I'll let him tell you. He asked me to bring you."

The world around her blurred as she followed Ezra to the car. She must have said goodbye to Theresa and the girls, but she couldn't remember it. She tried to get Ezra to give her more information on the drive to the hospital, but it was like talking to a brick wall.

"I'm sorry, Hilary. I promised Oliver I'd let him explain everything. But I can tell you that he's going to be okay."

She wasn't sure how long the drive took. Ezra parked at the hospital and led her through a maze of halls until they came to a cluster of people in a waiting room. Glancing around, she recognized several Coltons from having seen them at Atria. There were a few she didn't know, but the resemblance was enough to tell her they were part of Oliver's family as well.

Ezra stopped at a door and pushed it open, gesturing for her to enter first.

Hilary walked in to an argument in progress.

"—told you not to do anything stupid!"

"We got him, didn't we?"

Oliver sat in a hospital bed, his face bruised and

line of stitches along the curve of his jaw. He was frowning at his brother Dom, who stood glowering at him.

Dom glanced over and nodded at Ezra. "Good. Maybe you can get through to him."

Ezra closed the door. "Don't see the point," he replied. "What's done is done."

Hilary stared at Oliver, taking in his injuries. In addition to the bruises and scrapes on his face, his knuckles looked swollen and cut, and she could tell by the way he shifted that his body hurt.

Ignoring his brothers, she walked over to the bed. "What happened to you?" She reached for his hand, running her thumb across the reddened skin.

A guilty look flashed across his face. "It's not as bad as it looks," he said.

Alarm bells began to ring in her head. "That's not what I asked you."

Oliver sent a beseeching look to his brothers. She followed his gaze to see Dom and Ezra take a step back.

Dom held up his hands. "No way. I'm not getting in the middle of this. You acted a fool. Now you get to explain it."

The two men retreated into the hall, closing the door behind them.

"Cowards," Oliver muttered under his breath.

Hilary's concern took a back seat to her growing temper. "What did your brother mean by that comment? That you were a fool?"

"I did what had to be done—"

She held up a hand, impatience building in her chest. "I don't want excuses. I want you to tell me what happened to you. You were just supposed to go talk to the police about the blackmail and threats. How did you wind up in a hospital bed looking like death warmed over?"

Oliver sighed and began to talk, explaining how he'd cooperated with the police to set up a sting operation to incriminate Vince Doherty. The more he told her, the angrier Hilary grew.

She stood there, listening to him describe the meeting with Vince, the way he'd baited the man in an attempt to get him to say something the police could use against him. He'd lied to her, making her think he was simply going to the police station for an interview. That had been bad enough, but Oliver hadn't been content with goading Vince. No, he'd had to hit the man, wounding his pride along with his nose.

"So if the police had been even a moment later, you might have already been dead." She spoke quietly, not trusting her voice.

"I guess that's possible," he acknowledged. "But they weren't, so everything is okay."

She stared at him, fighting the urge to laugh. "Is that what you think?"

Oliver frowned. "What do you mean? Vince has been arrested. He's no longer a threat to us. We can move forward now, focus on the baby and our relationship."

It sounded so nice. For a second, Hilary wanted to agree with him. But she couldn't. Because it was clear that the kind of relationship Oliver wanted wasn't going to work for her.

The realization settled over her like a physical weight, making her knees buckle. She sank into a chair, shaking her head.

"Hilary?" Oliver sat up, clearly concerned. "Are you okay? Is it the baby?"

"No." She met his eyes, her body going numb as she spoke. "It's not the baby. It's you."

He frowned, his confusion plain. "I don't understand."

"I know you don't," she replied, her voice sounding flat even to her own ears. "I can tell you don't get it. I thought I made it clear to you that if we're going to work, you need to treat me like an equal partner, not an afterthought. It seemed like you understood and agreed with me, but it's clear you don't."

"Is this about the sting operation?" He started talking fast, as though he feared she would walk out before he'd fully explained himself. "I didn't want to worry you. You've been under so much stress already I didn't want to add to it."

"And you thought having your brother pick me up from the ranch to take me to see you in the hospital was a walk in the park?"

He had the sense to look embarrassed. "Not exactly. But—"

"Save it," she interrupted. "I don't want to hear any more excuses. We were supposed to be in this together. We were going to face this together and solve the problem as a team. But you cut me out. You decided to go off half-cocked without even consulting me about it. Instead, you lied to me."

"I didn't lie," he protested. "I told you I had a meeting with the police. I did."

"Don't try to split hairs now!" Hilary realized she had yelled and she took a deep breath, slipping the reins back on her temper. "I will not spend my life playing semantic games with you, Oliver Colton. You say you want a relationship with me, but your actions tell me otherwise. I deserve a partner who communicates freely and openly. Not a man who treats me like a business deal and uses language as a weapon to create loopholes for his behavior."

Oliver's face was pale. "What are you saying?"

"I'm saying I'm done." A chill raced over her as she spoke the words, her heart breaking with the acknowledgment.

"Hilary, no—"

She got to her feet, cutting him off. "I won't try to keep you from seeing the baby. I'm not a monster. But you and I are not going to happen." She started walking to the door, a little surprised her legs didn't give out as she moved.

"Hilary, I love you."

The words made her stop. She turned to face him, unable to stop the tears from flowing down her cheeks. "I thought you did," she replied. "But it's clear you don't know how to love me."

She pushed through the door, leaving Oliver alone in his room. She kept her head high as she walked past his siblings. They would take care of him. The Coltons always rallied to support each other.

Hopefully her family would do the same for her.

Chapter 17

Friday

Oliver winced as he climbed out of the rental car. The doctors had assured him that nothing had been permanently damaged as a result of his beating by Doherty's thugs, but he was still sore and aching from the experience.

He took the stairs to Hilary's apartment, walking slowly. No sense in arriving at her doorstep out of breath.

He'd done nothing but think about what she'd said in the two days that had passed since she'd walked out of his hospital room. At first, he'd been angry, incredulous that she had ended things so suddenly.

His only goal had been to keep her and the baby safe! Why hadn't she understood that?

But as time had passed, he'd started to see things from her perspective. He had kept her in the dark about his plans to deal with Vince. And he could see how he had lied to her, even though that hadn't been his intent.

Coming home to the empty suite had been depressing. Oliver had moped around, missing her. Missing the connection they had shared. Dom and Ezra had stopped by yesterday, trying to cheer him up. But Oliver wasn't in the mood to smile. Not while his heart was still in pieces.

Hilary hadn't answered his calls. Oliver knew he needed to give her space, but he just wanted to see her once more. It had been hard to explain everything in the hospital. Maybe now that they had both had a chance to calm down, they could try to talk again?

He'd packed up her things and carried the bag now as he approached her door. Nervous energy flowed through him, making his stomach churn and his heart pound. What if she didn't answer the door? What if she did answer, but took one look at him and shut it in his face? Only one way to know...

He pressed the doorbell and held his breath, waiting for some kind of response. Hilary had told him he could still be part of the baby's life; hopefully that meant she would still be willing to see him before the birth.

The lock moved with a *snick*. The door swung

open and there she was, looking so beautiful it made his chest constrict.

If she was surprised to see him, she didn't show it. "Hello."

"Hi," he breathed. He ran his eyes over her, drinking in the sight of her. Her eyes were clear, but he noticed the dark shadows underneath. Had she been having trouble sleeping again?

She shifted, the fabric of her shirt stretching across her belly. The bump appeared bigger, even though he'd seen her recently. His palm ached to touch her, to cradle their baby.

"Did you need something?"

Oliver realized he'd been staring at her. "Uh, I brought your things," He lifted the bag as he spoke. "Mind if I come in for a minute?"

Hilary nodded and stepped back.

He walked into her apartment, stepping into the living room. There was a cup of coffee on the table at the end of the sofa, making him think she'd been sitting there before he'd arrived.

"Where would you like this?" He held up the duffel again.

"I'll take it." She reached for the bag and placed it on the floor "Thanks for bringing it over."

"You're welcome."

Silence stretched between them, awkward and uncomfortable. "Can we sit?"

Hilary crossed her arms. "I'm not sure that's a good idea."

"Please?" he asked quietly. "I won't take too much of your time."

"All right." She sat next to the table and picked up the mug, cradling it in her hands.

Oliver took the chair to the side of her, leaning forward to face her.

"I've been thinking a lot about what you said the other day in the hospital. And you're right."

Surprise flickered across Hilary's face but she didn't respond.

"I wasn't including you in my decisions. I thought I was sparing you from more stress, but I see now I was keeping you in the dark because I didn't know how to handle your input."

She sucked in a breath. "You didn't want my opinion?"

Oliver tilted his head to the side. "That was part of it. I'm so used to doing things on my own, being the one to make decisions. The only people I've ever really relied on are Dom and Ezra. But now you're here, and I realize I don't want to do that anymore. I want to stand by you, to support you and have you support me. I want to be able to lean on you because I'm tired of going it alone."

"You know how I feel," she said softly. "How can I be sure you mean this? That you're not just saying it because of the baby?"

He took a chance, leaning over to reach for her hand. "I love you. I loved you before you got pregnant, and I'll love you after you have the baby. I'm not perfect, though—I'm going to make mistakes. But if you can see your way to trusting me and giving me another chance, I promise I will spend the rest of my life choosing you."

Tears welled in her eyes. "You have to talk to me," she said, her voice wobbly. "You can't just assume you know what's best for me. I don't need you to protect me, I need you to be honest with me."

Oliver nodded, his throat tight. "I realize that now. I never meant to hurt you. I thought I was doing the right thing by shielding you from the risks. But I know I would hate it if you did that to me. I was wrong and I'm sorry."

She nodded slowly. "No more loopholes?"

He shook his head. "No more loopholes." He squeezed her hand. "I just want you to love me again."

Hilary laughed. "I never stopped loving you."

Oliver's heart thumped hard against his ribs. "Really?"

She sniffed and dabbed at her nose with the back of her hand. "Of course not. I was angry and hurt and disappointed, but I still love you."

He moved to sit next to her on the sofa, unable to contain his smile. "You have no idea how relieved I am to hear you say that. I thought I'd lost you forever." He pulled her close for a hug. "I know I don't deserve you, but will you please give me another chance?"

"Yes," she said. "We've lost too much time already. I don't want to waste any more of it."

She kissed him then, a gesture of forgiveness, a promise of their future.

A reminder of their love.

Oliver wrapped his arms around her, his heart seeming to expand as it filled with love. He didn't have to be alone anymore. He'd found his person, the woman who was perfect for him. And even though the path to her hadn't always been smooth or straight, they were together now.

He didn't know what troubles the future might hold. But one thing was certain: they would face them side by side.

As partners.

Epilogue

"Are you ready to see your baby?" The technician smiled as Hilary lifted the hem of her shirt to expose her belly.

"Yes." She and Oliver spoke at the same time, both of them equally excited for this moment.

She laughed as he took her hand. They had spent the weekend talking, getting to know each other on a deeper level. Fortunately, everything she had learned about Oliver had only made her love him more. She'd never felt so close to another person, and now that they were determined to make things work between them, she knew she'd always have a partner as they moved through life together.

The technician tucked a paper drape into the

waistband of Hilary's pants. "The gel should be nice and warm for you," she said, squirting some onto Hilary's skin. Then she applied the ultrasound probe and started moving it around.

Hilary squinted at the screen, trying to make sense of the images. To her untrained eyes, the gray and white looked like the jumbled signal of a TV station that was out of service. But the technician seemed to know what she was doing. She moved the wand around Hilary's belly quickly, pressing here, gliding over that spot. Just as Hilary began to make out what she was seeing, the wand moved again, zooming over to a different spot.

She glanced up at Oliver, wondering if he was having any luck picking out features. But based on his frown, he didn't seem to recognize anything, either.

"Hmm." The technician's utterance was not reassuring. "I'll be right back," she said, putting the wand down. "I'm just going to grab your doctor."

"Wait, what's wrong?" But she was out the door before Hilary could finish speaking.

Her anxiety shot through the roof. There was a problem with the baby—why else would the technician leave so suddenly? But what was wrong? Was it a condition that could be treated, or was it fatal for the fetus?

Hilary's eyes welled with tears and her breathing quickened. Oliver squeezed her hand and she looked up as he leaned over her.

"It's going to be okay," he said, using his free hand to push her hair off her cheek. "Whatever it is, we'll face it together and we'll figure out a way forward."

She nodded, unable to speak.

"Deep breaths," he said softly. "The doctor will be here soon and we'll know what's going on."

"Why didn't she tell me?" Surely if everything was okay the technician would have said as much?

"She's not supposed to," Oliver said. "Remember, only the doctor is allowed to talk about what the ultrasound shows."

He was right; she knew that, and yet she couldn't hold back her tears.

Oliver dragged a chair over to the side of the bed and sat, his arms circling her as best he could. Hilary gripped his hand like a lifeline, his quiet strength keeping her from completely falling apart.

After a seemingly endless stretch of minutes, there was a short knock and the doctor entered.

She took one look at Hilary's face and stepped closer. "The technician didn't see anything abnormal," she said. "But there is something she wanted me to verify."

Hilary's breath gusted out, leaving her feeling hollow and shaky. Oliver squeezed her hand in silent reassurance. "Okay," she said, her voice wobbly with residual emotion.

The doctor smiled and took a seat, then donned gloves and picked up the ultrasound wand. She placed it on Hilary's belly and began to scan.

"Oh. Yes, the tech was right."

"What's going on?" Oliver asked. His voice was calm but Hilary heard the note of strain and knew he shared her worry.

"I'll show you," the doctor replied. "This right here is baby A." She held the wand in position and a small figure came into view. Hilary was able to make out a large head and what looked like a spine. "Here's the heart," the doctor continued, moving the wand slightly. A small flickering caught her eye, and she realized with a small shock she was seeing her baby's heartbeat.

"Oh my gosh," she murmured. She'd never seen anything so amazing before!

Oliver's breath caught. "That's incredible," he murmured.

The doctor smiled. "Pretty cool, right?"

Hilary nodded. "Now, here's what the technician noticed earlier." She moved the wand again, sliding it to the left before stopping.

Hilary squinted at the screen. "Is this a different view?"

"Nope." The doctor's eyes glinted with mischief. "It's a different baby!"

"What?" A shock rippled through her body as the doctor's words sank in. "Are you saying…"

"Twins!" the woman confirmed.

Hilary glanced up at Oliver. He looked as dumbstruck as she felt. After a few seconds, he threw back his head and started laughing.

"Of course," he said, shaking his head with a smile. "Why stop at one when we could have two?"

The doctor continued the exam, pointing out hands and legs and bellies. "And let me see…yep, we can definitely tell the sexes. Do you want to know?"

"I do." Hilary replied. "What about you?"

Oliver nodded. "Definitely. I like to be prepared."

"I don't blame you," the doctor said. "Okay, then. Baby A looks like a girl, and baby B is a boy. You get one of each!"

Joy spread through Hilary, the warmth chasing away the last of her earlier concerns. Two babies. Both healthy and strong. She couldn't ask for more.

The doctor wrapped up the exam and printed off pictures for them. Then she wiped the gel from Hilary's belly and sent them back into the waiting room. "The nurse will call you back again soon for the rest of your appointment."

Hilary and Oliver sat next to each other. The doctor had managed to get profile shots of both babies, and they pored over them now. It was too soon to see any family resemblance, but that didn't stop them from trying to find one.

"Did you ever think it would be twins?" he asked, an awestruck expression on his face.

Hilary shook her head. "One baby was surprise enough," she joked. "But at least we won't be outnumbered!"

He laughed. "True. Now we just have to agree on names."

"Actually, I've been thinking about that," she said. "Remember when you told me about your work and I called you a green Robin Hood?"

"I do." His eyes sparkled with amusement.

"I've always liked the name Robin," Hilary continued. "What do you think about Robin and Marian?"

Oliver's smile broadened. "I love it."

"You do?" She hadn't expected them to settle on a name so quickly, much less two names!

"I do," he confirmed. He leaned over and kissed her. "And I love you."

"I love you, too." There wasn't anyone she'd rather go on this journey with, and no one she could imagine better suited to help her raise twins. He was her rock, her safe place.

Seeing the images of their babies, feeling her heart grow with each second she spent memorizing their features, Hilary realized Oliver had given her more than his love.

He'd given her the world.

* * * * *

#2199 COLTON'S ROGUE INVESTIGATION
The Coltons of Colorado • by Jennifer D. Bokal

Wildlife biologist Jacqui Reyes is determined to find out who's trying to steal the wild mustangs of western Colorado. She enlists the help of true-crime podcaster, Gavin Colton. He's working on a series about his notorious father but he can't help but be drawn into Jacqui's case—or toward Jacqui herself!

#2200 CAVANAUGH JUSTICE: DEADLIEST MISSION
Cavanaugh Justice • by Marie Ferrarella

When his sister goes missing, small-town sheriff Cody Cassidy races to her home in Aurora. All he finds is heartbreak...and the steady grace of Detective Skylar Cavanaugh. Once firmly on the track of a killer, Cody and Skylar discover they have more in common than crime. But a murderer is on a killing spree that threatens their budding relationship.

#2201 PROTECTED BY THE TEXAS RANCHER
by Karen Whiddon

Rancher Trace Adkins is wary when Emma McBride shows up on his doorstep. How could he let a woman convicted of murdering her husband into his home? But he's never believed in her guilt, and the simmering attraction he's always felt toward her remains. Despite his misgivings, he agrees to let her stay until she gets on her feet, unaware that someone is after her.

#2202 REUNION AT GREYSTONE MANOR
by Bonnie Vanak

Going back to his hometown is painful, but FBI agent Roarke Calhoun has inherited a mansion, which will help save a life in crisis. But returning means facing Megan Robinson, the woman he's always loved. She also has a claim on the mansion, which puts them together in a place full of secret dangers...and a love meant to burn hot.

Was she really considering allowing herself to be
captured by the man who'd killed Amber? Even though
he'd insisted he hadn't murdered Jeremy, how did she
know for sure? She could be putting herself into the
hands of a ruthless monster.

The sound of the back door opening cut into her
thoughts.

"Hey there," Trace said, dropping into the chair next
to her, one lock of his dark hair falling over his forehead.
He looked so damn handsome her chest ached. "Are you
okay? You look upset."

If he only knew.

"Maybe a little," she admitted, well aware he'd see straight through her if she tried to claim she wasn't. In the short time they'd been together, she couldn't help but notice how attuned he'd become to her emotions. And she to his. Suddenly, she understood that if she really was going to go through with this risky plan, she wanted to make love to Trace one last time.

Moving quickly, before she allowed herself to doubt or rationalize, she turned to him. "I need you," she murmured, getting up and moving over to sit on his lap. His gaze darkened as she wrapped her arms around him. When she leaned in close and grazed her mouth across his, he met her kiss with the kind of blazing heat that made her lose all sense of rhyme or reason.

Don't miss
Protected by the Texas Rancher *by Karen Whiddon,*
available October 2022 wherever
Harlequin Romantic Suspense books and
ebooks are sold.

Harlequin.com

HRSEXP0822